TRISTAN
ON A HARLEY

(A LOUISIANA KNIGHTS NOVEL)

Jennifer

Blake

SMP

STEEL MAGNOLIA PRESS

TRISTAN ON A HARLEY

Copyright © 2016 Patricia Maxwell

Cover Art by Croco Designs

For more information contact:
patriciaamaxwell@bellsouth.net

ISBN: 9781519063786

To-morrow, and to-morrow, and to-morrow,
Creeps in this petty pace from day to day,
To the last syllable of recorded time;
And all our yesterdays have lighted fools
The way to dusty death. Out, out, brief candle!
Life's but a walking shadow, a poor player,
That struts and frets his hour upon the stage,
And then is heard no more. It is a tale
Told by an idiot, full of sound and fury,
Signifying nothing.

Macbeth Act V, Scene 5, 19–28

CHAPTER ONE

"What's going on?"

Zeni Medford jumped a little, startled, as that deep-voiced question came from behind her. She turned from the front window of the Watering Hole coffee shop and restaurant, where she'd been watching a long line of vehicles pass by, led by a police car with flashing lights. She'd thought she was alone, since the usual customers were all standing out on the street for a better view.

Her boss, Trey Benedict, shifted position, moving so close that her bare arm, exposed by her tomato red tank top, brushed his elbow. The voltage that flashed between them was so strong she felt it down to her toes. It wasn't fair. In fact, it was downright annoying that he still had that effect upon her after more than two years of working together.

"What does it look like?" she answered with scant grace. "An invasion by aliens in black limos?" Trey squinted at the parade of vehicles heading toward the courthouse square. "And maybe a convention for monster motor homes."

"It's the movie people, of course. Where have you been that you don't know?"

"Colorado mountain back trails. Not much news from sleepy old Chamelot lately."

Zeni's question had been completely rhetorical. She always knew where Trey was and what he was doing. On top of that, she'd been dutifully holding down the fort at the coffee shop, also looking after the convenience stores and truck stop he owned, while he'd been away at the High Rockies dirt bike competition.

She hadn't realized he was back. No reason she should, of course; he had a house outside town, and came and went as he pleased. She didn't expect him to check in with her. It might've been nice, but it wasn't happening.

"I suppose you won," she said.

"Not this time. Might have, except I crashed, had to stop and repair the bike in the middle of a lightning storm."

"Going too fast as usual." Busting his chops was a reflex action, but better than having him guess at how her stomach muscles clenched from the thought of him riding head-first into a tree, or maybe flying off the side of some slippery mountain trail.

"One of the old hands told me that if you don't crash at least twice every lap you're not going fast enough."

"Did he now?" she asked with cool irony. "With an attitude like that, I'm surprised he ever got to be an old hand."

The look he gave her was jaundiced, but without heat. The surprise for him would probably have been if she'd had no quick comeback. One day she was going to shock him and say what she really thought.

Yeah, sure she was.

"What movie is this?" he asked, turning back to the sun-drenched outside view, peering over the Watering Hole's lettering on the glass. "And what people?"

"An L.A. outfit doing a romantic comedy. The producer/director is the big western star, Derek Peabody, who will also be playing the male lead."

"Ambitious of him."

"He's apparently managed it before. That's him and his entourage arriving now, minus the leading lady who will show up later. The word is he'll be holding a cattle call in a couple of days."

She gave Trey a brief sidelong glance, noting the damp, close-cropped waves of his hair that were dark brown but looked black in the dim light, the thick fans of his lashes that almost hid the gray of his eyes, and the square jaw with its two-day scruff of beard. He'd stopped long enough to shower before coming on to the coffee shop; the only scents she caught with her quick and stealthy inhalation were soap, fabric softener, and healthy male.

"A what?"

"Casting call is the official name," she answered. "It's a roundup of people from around town who aren't actors but may be hired as extras for crowd scenes. The whole town's learning movie lingo, you know."

"And I guess you plan on being at this call up, or whatever it is?"

She lifted a shoulder. "Haven't really thought about it."

"Don't waste your time."

"What's that supposed to mean?" Rounding on him, she was distracted for an instant by the heat that radiated from his body, invading her very bones.

"I doubt you're the type they're after. They'll want folks who look normal."

"Normal?"

The edge she put on that single word could have sliced through a steel cable. She wasn't exactly bland and ordinary, but neither was she abnormal. That Trey could hint at such a thing was surprising. He might give as good as he got in their exchanges, but he wasn't usually mean about it.

"Now don't get on your high horse—I'm just saying you'd stand out too much in a crowd." His gaze lingered a second on her long, wavy hair that she'd dyed grape juice purple the night before and pulled up into twin pony tails that stuck out on top of her head like cow horns this morning, also her hoop earrings the size of cereal bowls and the small gold ring in her right nostril. "You don't exactly fade into the background, you know."

Of course she didn't; she never had and never would. "Why would anyone want to do that?"

"To catch a casting director's eye, that's why. They don't want extras that draw attention and maybe distract the audience from what's going on with the main actors."

Zeni made a disparaging sound. "As if I could go that far."

"You might, and it's enough to get you disqualified."

That sounded a little better than what he'd said before, though she wasn't about to let him know it. "You understand all this, being such an expert on the movie business."

"I've read a thing or two."

"So have I. And I'm sure I could be as average as the next person if necessary."

The look he gave her was searching. She could almost feel it skimming over her smooth, tanned skin, the width of her forehead, the wide spacing of her oversized brown eyes with their seven shades of eye makeup and goddess design drawn in henna, the straight slope of her nose and curves of her lips. Her breathing lost its easy rhythm, while her heartbeat kicked up a notch.

Endless seconds later, a wry smile tugged at one corner of his mouth. "Nah. You're just too different. Besides, I'd have thought showing up for this call would be the last thing you'd do."

"It might have been before you started in on the way I look," she answered smartly.

He took a deep breath and let it out. "I was just making a comment, not saying you should change. You just—you're you."

"In other words, not like everybody else." She wouldn't let the pain of that show; the result from such weakness was something she'd faced ages ago.

"Well, yeah, but I thought you liked it that way. You go to a lot of trouble to make sure of it."

He was right in a way. The reasons she did that were many—to avoid boring expectations, to express how she felt inside, to show people she didn't care what they thought, to live close to the edge. And yet it all boiled down to the same thing, didn't it? She wanted to be different, just not in the same way she'd been all her life.

Different had been good for a while. Now it wasn't, not really. The question was whether she could find an acceptable reason to change.

She'd always been a freak, the child genius in math and science who made up a father because she had none, the daughter who sometimes frightened her mother with what she knew though she was also her best friend; the nerdy kid who handled the family finances from age six, and was so engrossed in her studies by sixteen that she barely noticed boys were on the planet. The girl who at 17 woke up one morning to discover that her mother had died in the night of an unsuspected aneurysm, leaving her alone in the world.

"That was before," she said, her voice hard. "This is now." And she wasn't entirely sure whether she was answering her own thoughts or what Trey had said.

"You really might try out?"

He sounded disapproving as well as disbelieving. She could see only one reason for that. "If you think I'd neglect my job—"

"Not at all," he said before she could finish. "You enjoy it, and you're good at it. I just hate to see you disappointed."

"I'm a big girl," she said with her most deadly stare, the one that usually said any caffeine-or-alcohol-laden jerk who dared grab any part of her might draw back a nub. "I can take it."

"But still."

"Still what? You don't think I have a chance of being chosen? You're so sure of it you're feeling sorry for me already?"

"I'm not, no. All I'm saying is it doesn't seem like something you'd enjoy. You're not much for pretending."

That's what he thought, Zeni told herself. And a good thing it was, too.

Trey had Zeni hemmed in, though she didn't seem to realize it. A table with its four chairs sat at an angle behind her, forming a corner. The way he stood facing her closed off the open side. He could have moved, but wasn't so inclined. He liked being in control for these few brief minutes. It was such a rarity, after all.

She could push past him at any time, of course. His superiority was all a mental game, one he played with no one except Zeni. Using physical strength against women wasn't his style.

Zeni didn't seem to mind his closeness, or maybe it was just that she failed to notice it, which was a definite downer. Her attention had been reclaimed by events beyond the window. The longer of the limos had pulled up at the street's end. The mayor of Chamelot was descending the steps of the columned courthouse, hand outstretched to greet the visitors, flashing her whitened smile and wearing her best convention-going green suit that was a rather obvious complement to her red hair.

The guy who stepped from the limo was average in height with the ripped appearance provided by a personal trainer, home gym and unlimited time. His California blond hair and tan were both a little too perfect to be natural and the designer who provided his wardrobe too body-conscious, judging by the close fit of his shirt and pants. His sunglasses flashed dollar signs in the sun, and it was a toss-up which was shinier, his silk ascot or his patent leather shoes. He moved with languid steps, or as if it was beneath him to meet the mayor halfway. Barely touching the hand she offered, he waved his minions forward to be introduced, removing the necessity of making nice with the town officials.

Trey disliked him on sight.

"Who's the big-wig again?" he asked in a tone like a slow ride over new gravel.

"Derek Peabody," Zeni said without taking her eyes from the man. "He was the star of a western series that ran forever, *Fiery Six-Shooters*, or something like that."

"*Rifle Fire?*" he ventured.

"That's the one. It's amazing that he chose Chamelot as the location for this production."

She had a point. The sleepy old river town of barely 3,000 souls wasn't exactly a film-making mecca, unlike other cities across the South. But Trey wasn't about to agree with her.

"Not so amazing. I seem to remember when her honor, the mayor, met him at that big film festival in New Orleans—she couldn't talk about anything else for a month. She must have given away most of Chamelot to get him here."

Zeni gave him a quick glance over one shoulder. "She's promised full cooperation from every business, including the Watering Hole."

"Say what?"

"We are to provide food for the cast and crew while they're out on location."

"Funny," Trey drawled, "but I don't remember agreeing to that."

"You didn't," she said with a snort, unimpressed by his obvious displeasure. "I did."

"What?"

"You should have been here, instead of plowing through mud and rocks out on a dirt track."

It was a job, holding onto his temper, but he managed it. "Do you have any idea how much that's going to cost? Or how we'll manage it without hiring more help?"

"I think Gloria and I can handle it," she said, naming the college girl who'd started helping out part time when they changed from being a coffee shop only to serving beer and wine with restaurant-type meals. "And it's not like we'll be doing it for free; the movie company will pay. Any extra cost will be offset by the food and drink the movie people pick up here when not actively shooting the film. It's not as if there are a lot of other places in Chamelot for them to eat or relax."

She had the finances covered; he should have known. Still, he couldn't help rattling her chain. "On the other hand, good old Derek may hire buses to take them to New Orleans for their meals and R&R."

"Don't be such a pessimist."

"Somebody has to think about these things. What about the medieval fair? It seems to me this movie crew will be in the way when people start to gather for it."

"I heard the fair is one of the reasons Chamelot was chosen as a location, that some of the events may be used in the movie. It'll all work out, you'll see. Besides, it's not as if we have a movie crew in town every day."

"Thank heaven for small mercies."

"What was that?" she asked, turning to look at him, the rich dark brown of her eyes like the most decadent of boutique chocolates.

"I said thank heaven you're taking care of it, because I won't be around," he said in sturdy defense against his too vivid imagination.

"Sure you will."

He should have known better than to shoot off his mouth with an empty threat. Zeni knew him too well to believe he'd be anywhere else with this kind of business in the offing. "At least it settles one thing."

She lifted a brow that had rust-red squiggles drawn under it. "And that would be?"

"You'll be so busy there won't be time for playing at being an extra."

"You think so, do you?"

"Stands to reason." He refused to back down; pride and sanity demanded that he hold his own.

"I don't see why, when you'll be around to take up the slack." She crossed her arms over her chest, a move that did things to the neckline of her tank top that should be against the law.

"Now, Zeni—" he began.

"It has nothing to do with coping, does it? You don't want me to have anything to do with the movie people."

"It's not that."

"What, then? I'll be an embarrassment to Chamelot?"

"Don't be ridiculous!"

"You don't think I can do it. You don't believe I can fit in with the rest, be selected at this cattle call. You think I'll be back here with my tail between my legs, and you don't want to deal with it."

"Oh, for pity's sake." Trey looked away out the window, staring at the styled-up actor/director without seeing him. Zeni was right, but it was because he didn't want to see her stripped of all her feisty bravado by disappointment, especially if it was handed out by that phony in the shiny shoes. Trey couldn't stand the thought of it, though why that might be was something he didn't care to examine too closely.

"I can, you know."

"But why would you want to?"

"To prove it's possible. What do you want to bet that's

what happens?"

"Nothing," he answered in grim finality. "You don't have to prove a thing to me."

"I think I do. Tell you what—if I'm one of the chosen, you'll do whatever I tell you for a solid day, and if I'm not—"

"You're kidding, right?"

"Why would you think that?"

That was an easy one. He couldn't feature her wanting to spend a whole day with him, much less have any reason for ordering him around. No matter, he knew how to put a stop to this line of talk.

"And if you aren't, if you don't get to be an extra, I get the same privilege you're claiming?"

Her lashes flickered before she answered. "I guess. But you get to tell me what to do all the time anyway."

"It won't be the same thing at all." He gave her his sexiest grin. Zeni was a smart cookie. She wouldn't walk into the kind of open-ended personal danger he was half-threatening.

Or would she?

She studied him for long moments while the autumn sunlight bouncing from the street outside filtered through her hair, giving it the appearance of spun filaments of grape candy. It touched her eyes and shone on the burgundy red gloss on her lips. Unbidden thoughts of hot chocolate sundaes drenched in cherry syrup swirled in his head.

Her lashes came down, concealing her thoughts. When she answered, he felt the force of it like a sucker punch.

"If that's the way you want it."

She didn't intend to lose the bet; that much was clear. But if she did, then yes, he did indeed want a whole day of telling her what to do. He wanted to say so, but the possibilities of his inevitable win stunned him into mute stupidity.

"Well?" she demanded.

He cleared his throat, gave a jerky nod. "You're on."

"Yeah?"

He met her gaze, absorbing the surprise there while a fierce brand of exhilaration rose inside him. "Yeah," he answered. "Oh, yeah."

CHAPTER TWO

*T*he gathering place for the cattle call was in the largest exhibit building at the old fairgrounds, the site of the annual agricultural fair that had fallen to the wayside in recent years. Much of the area had been allotted to the movie company for the duration, though a portion was reserved for the medieval fair.

When Zeni walked into the cavernous building, people were milling around, visiting, waiting for things to get started. Their voices bounced from the polished floor to the high ceiling and back again; some were high-pitched with excitement, while others were laden with half-humorous curiosity. Though a few might have visions of movie stardom, most were on hand simply to see what was going on. No one seemed to have any idea of how these try-outs were supposed to work, when they would get started, or how long they would last.

The day was warm, even if it was October. Although the big double doors of the old building stood open, the ever-increasing crowd compounded the heat. Zeni fanned herself with the event brochure that she'd picked up just inside the door and looked around, smiling and nodding at Watering Hole customers she recognized here and there. There were quite a few, actually; it was a constant amazement, the number of people she met at the coffee shop, all of whom seemed to remember her.

She still wasn't used to being memorable in a physical sense, although she'd gone to great lengths over the past couple of years to stand out, even getting a large tattoo across her back. It was infinitely better than being a bore, remembered only for a freaky ability with numbers and Trivial Pursuit.

"Hi, girlfriend! That slave-driver of a boss let you off for a change?"

That greeting came from Mandy Benedict, wife of Tunica Parish's sheriff. A quick hug came with it; Mandy was still in the honeymoon phase after just over a year of marriage, so she loved everybody.

Zeni returned the hug with gusto. She adored Mandy and her husband. That she'd had a role in bringing the two of them together was a source of quirky pride.

"So, are you trying out as an extra?" she asked.

"Why not?" Mandy asked with laughter sparkling in the sea blue of her eyes and a shake of her head that made gold-brown curls dance around an expressive face. "What else do I have to do? Not that it's a make-or-break deal in my life, but I figure I can walk across the street as well as anybody."

"Exactly, and better than most." Zeni paused. "You have any idea what the movie is supposed to be about?"

"An oddball thing full of Southern angst, weird dream sequences and football as far as I can tell."

"You're kidding. I heard it was a comedy."

"Well, sort of. It's billed as *Superman* meets *She*, if you can believe it. The basic idea is a football hero desperately in love with a sophisticated woman, but who can't get her to even look his way. After he performs some heroic deed and gains her respect, he realizes the woman is too coldhearted for him. He prefers his fantasy world where every woman he meets is hot for him and asks for it outright."

"Sounds like a fantasy, all right. So then what happens?"

"That's anybody's guess, apparently, which seems to be the deal with making movies. By the time everyone from the director to the lead actor adds their input, the original writer can't recognize his own script."

"And the actor/director here has total control?"

"Exactly. It will work out however Derek Peabody decides, when the time comes."

"I don't suppose we care, as long as we get to walk across the street with everybody else," Zeni said with a laugh.

"Our moment of glory, immortalized on film. It's about the most any of us can hope for, right?"

"More than likely," Zeni agreed, though she knew Sheriff Lancelot Benedict's wife was being overly modest. Mandy might be a new mom to four-month-old Caleb, but she was a town powerhouse. A sponsor for the annual Relay for Life, on the boards of both the annual pilgrimage of homes and the library, initiator of a future river park for kids, and founder of a safe house for women and children escaping domestic abuse, she was always up to something. Give her another year or two, and she'd either be mayor—not an impossibility as Chamelot had a female mayor already— or there would be a statue of her erected in front of the courthouse.

"Where's Lance this morning?" Zeni asked, scanning the crowd. He was sure to be around somewhere for this kind of event.

"The poor dear is directing traffic out at the highway. You wouldn't believe the people in town today, every single one of them circling, circling to find the best parking place for this event because they don't want to walk a single step more than necessary."

"I know he loves that," Zeni said with a grin. She hadn't seen him because she'd walked from the Watering Hole. One reason she'd settled in Chamelot was because her old rattletrap of a car had given up the ghost at the city limits.

"Yeah, not his favorite part of the job. And he already had smoke coming out of his ears after a run-in with the man of the hour earlier."

Zeni swung back toward Mandy. "Derek Peabody, you mean?"

"None other. He seems to think he can take over the town, park his limo anywhere he pleases. Unfortunately, he appropriated Judge Martin's parking space on the court-house square, along with three or four others. You can imagine how that went over."

"The judge wasn't happy?"

"He told Peabody to move his limo or it would be towed. I'm not sure how that was answered, but the next thing you know, the judge was threatening to bloody the guy's cosmetically enhanced nose for him with one hand while dialing Lance's office with the other."

"Wow."

"Things simmered down once Lance arrived and it became clear the full judicial power of the district court could be brought to bear. Derek Peabody and his chauffeur decided they didn't need to take up a whole row of spaces after all."

"What did Lance think of him? Did he say?"

"Not in so many words," Mandy answered with a definite quirk to her mouth. "But he was wearing his grim look, which tells me he expects nothing good during these next few weeks. My guess is, he thinks Derek Peabody is a pain in the rear."

That last word was almost drowned out by a sudden rise in conversational volume around them. It started near the door and came toward them in a wave. The crowd shifted, people craning their necks or standing on tiptoe to see.

"Looks as if things are about to get underway," Zeni said.

They were indeed. Chamelot's lady mayor and the actor/director were moving slowly through the crowd. As they reached center stage, the mayor raised her arms in an appeal for quiet. When the noise died away, she began her little speech. She was delighted to see everyone coming out to support this movie venture, the first in what she hoped would be many more. It was her great honor to introduce the man who was going to bring fame and fortune to Chamelot, one who would showcase their traditions while making clear the special nature of the town. They would be offering hospitality for several weeks to the people working on the film, and she hoped everyone would join with her in making their stay a pleasant one. She gave them the star of Puma Films, Derek Peabody.

The crowd broke into enthusiastic applause. The actor/director quelled it with upraised hands. He was pleased by his reception in Chamelot and looked forward to filming his latest and greatest find, the dramatic comedy *Brief Candles*, based loosely on the famous soliloquy from *Macbeth*, among its good people. Waving forward a statuesque blonde in a dark pantsuit and four-inch stilettos, he introduced her as his personal assistant and co-producer, Bettina, whom he was sure everyone would come to know and love in the days ahead. Other cast members and production staff were also introduced and dismissed. With these preliminaries out of the way, he proceeded to organize those standing around as if his every second was precious beyond words.

Maybe it was, as time was money in the film industry. Or so Zeni had heard.

The crowd was separated into groups of men, women and children, and all of them lined up in separate rows. Derek Peabody then walked along the lines with his personal assistant on his heels. As one person and then another was selected, the assistant paused to take down names and contact information in her expensive looking portfolio with a clipboard.

Among those singled out were Granny Chauvin, looking her usual wise-old-owl self in a nice pastel suit and pretty blouse; young Lizzie Masters and her mom; and Carla Benedict, Trey's cousin Beau's new wife, who gave her a mock queenly wave from further down the line of women. A trio of older men were chosen, one of whom was former Sheriff Tate, the man Lance had defeated in the last election; he'd been tapped for what sounded like a checker game in front of the feed and hardware store. Up and down the actor/director went, picking people from no more than a whim, or so it appeared, though Bettina, trailing behind him, murmured to him now and then.

On their third pass along the rows, the duo stopped in front of Mandy. The assistant, towering over her boss by a good two inches in her heels, stooped to whisper in his ear. He nodded. The female assistant stepped close to take down Mandy's phone number while saying something about a dance scene.

When the pair turned their attention to her, Zeni thought for sure she was about to be selected. She could have smiled, maybe been at least a little ingratiating, but she refused. It wasn't in her nature, for one thing, but she also didn't care enough about a part to openly try for it. The acceleration of her heartbeat was at the prospect of winning her bet with Trey.

Looking past the pair, she met Mandy's eyes for a

minute, seeing the gleeful anticipation in them as the sheriff's wife gave her a wink. It was all Zeni could do not to
answer it.

The female assistant leaned in for a brief consultation.
Derek Peabody frowned. The two of them moved on.

Zeni's disappointment at being passed over was stronger
than she'd anticipated. She'd thought she was immune, but
for a moment she was that weird girl—the one who was
never chosen for the softball team, asked to birthday parties
or invited to school dances. With resolution, she pushed
those old hurts aside and focused on the present. It was
going to be pure hell, facing Trey with the news. He would
be merciless about it, she was sure. There was no telling
what he would find for her to do as payoff for their bet.

He could be clever about that kind of thing, at least
whenever it involved one of his male cousins. She had managed to avoid being on the losing side of a dispute with him
to this point, but that was in the past.

For a brief few seconds, she thought back to the terms of
their bet. What had she said, exactly? That he would have to
do whatever she told him for a solid day? She'd planned
things for him such as washing dishes behind the coffee
shop counter or cleaning out the big garbage cans in the
back, but she didn't believe that's what he'd had in mind
when he agreed to her terms.

A shiver ran over her, leaving goose bumps in its wake,
as she considered the possibilities. She could be in a lot of
trouble. And it wasn't that she'd be reluctant to comply with
whatever he demanded. No, not at all. The problem was

that she might be all too willing.

She'd been at great pains to keep her distance from Trey. He was bad news for someone like her. For all his bad boy reputation and biker lifestyle on the weekends, he was a Benedict, which made him Chamelot aristocracy. He wouldn't want someone like her. He'd want the whole sweet Southern Belle package, a woman who could sing in the church choir on Sunday, plan a dinner party on Wednesday, step out in style on Saturday evening, and be pleasantly submissive in his bed every other night of the week.

That wasn't her, and Zeni knew it. No way, no how.

Oh, she didn't doubt he'd take her to bed if she acted at all interested. But she'd watched her mom go that route, watched her get her heart broken too many times. More than that, she'd gone to bed for one-nighters with a couple of guys. She'd thought that would be enough at the time, but it wasn't. She needed something more. And if she couldn't have it, she wanted nothing at all. Even from Trey. Especially from Trey.

"What happened?" Mandy asked in a quiet undertone as she stepped closer. "I thought for sure you were about to be chosen."

"You've got me." Zeni lifted one shoulder in a would-be careless shrug that didn't quite make it. "I guess they just didn't like the way I looked."

Trey knew being chosen as an extra wasn't in the cards for

Zeni almost as soon as she did. Not that he was on hand. Though he could have discovered it himself by hanging out at the old exhibition hall, he wanted nothing to do with that scene. Rather, half a dozen people who had been there made a fast exit ahead of the crowd and came by the coffee shop to give him the lowdown.

Relief poured over him at the news. She'd be avoiding the movie crowd now, which was a good thing. More than that, he hadn't much cared for the look in Zeni's eyes as she'd put her challenge to him. He'd shifted a bucket load of his responsibilities onto her slender shoulders in the past few months, and figured he was about to be paid back for it.

It was possible she had something a bit more personal in mind, but he doubted it. She'd been wary around him from her first day at work, displaying a hands-off attitude that she reinforced with prickly put-downs. They'd been fairly mild at first, but were getting more snarky every week.

He got a kick out of teasing her until she gave him the sharp edge of her tongue. She made it almost irresistible with her hot reactions, but he knew better than to go too far. Some women had "I'm available" smiles and glances; others had expressions that said "Go away and leave me alone." With Zeni, he got the message. And since he didn't want to lose her, liked having her around, plus wasn't sure how he'd run his different business interests without her, he paid attention.

He was in the back storeroom, at the table that they used for breaks, when she came through the rear door. He didn't intend to provide a free show for customers, even if he couldn't wait to crow about her losing the bet she'd proposed. It wasn't his style, and certainly wasn't Zeni's.

"Just a second," he said, looking up from the legal pad where he'd been scribbling. "I almost have my list of jobs ready for you."

"I'll just bet you do." Zeni hung her shoulder bag on a hook beside the back entrance and took down one of her aprons that hung there, one made of denim to match the skirt she always wore, but dressed up with a huge green velvet flower, ribbons, silver chains and Mardi Gras beads. "Don't worry. There's nothing on it you wouldn't ask from me."

"I'm not worried."

"Good. You won't mind starting with a massage then, will you?"

"A massage." The look she gave him should have killed him stone-cold-dead, and might have if he hadn't been ready for it.

"Full body. With or without clothes," he said, keeping his face straight with an effort. "I'm not bashful."

He'd never seen her turn quite that red before. Amazing. Her lips darkened to the color of black raspberries, and her eyes grew as hot and meltingly dark as lava cakes. The golden tan skin of her face looked warm to the touch, and he could see the throb of her pulse in her neck.

The need to put his mouth to that gentle pulsing gave him a starving feeling inside, and the urge to turn her into dessert then and there was so strong he felt his eyes water.

"Well, I am!" she snapped, and headed past him, jerking

the door into the coffee shop open so hard and fast it flew out of her hand and slammed into the wall.

"Or you could start by polishing my boots!" he called after her. "I ran through a big puddle on my last ride, and they're muddy!"

Zeni didn't answer, which was probably best. She could say things that cut to the bone when she wanted, and he'd come close to being sliced and diced there for a second. Probably the only thing that kept him from it was that she knew she'd walked into this deal with her eyes open.

He'd figured she'd be disappointed after being passed over by the actor guy when even Granny Chauvin had been picked for a street scene. His intention was to distract her, make her irritated enough she'd forget about it, even if her anger was directed at him.

Big mistake. Now he had to fix it.

Trey glanced down at his list that actually had things on it such as going out to dinner with him, making him a grilled cheese sandwich for lunch, and helping him take photos of the antiques in his granddad's old place so they could be appraised for insurance. As mad as she was just now, he might have to hide the knives until she cooled down. With a quick shake of his head, he uncoiled from his chair and moved after her.

The main room of the Watering Hole was packed, not unusual when anything special was happening in town. Folks gravitated there to wind down with coffee and a piece of one of Zeni's amazing pies with the sky-high meringue on top. The fillings varied according to some plan Trey had never quite been able to make out, but thought probably had more to do with her mood than the ingredients in the store room. Today, the choices were chocolate, coconut and lemon custard, the best he remembered.

The part-time help, Gloria—young and on track for an advanced degree through online classes—had been behind the counter earlier. Now she'd been sent out to wait on customers and man the cash register while Zeni took over as short-order cook. Trey lifted a brow at the sight of his mad female manager cutting pies into even slices with a chef's knife the size of a machete, but kept his doubts and opinions to himself.

"Trey! Over here!"

He changed directions at that hail, wending his way through the tables to the corner where his two cousins, Lance and Beau, sat. He saw at a glance that they had coffee and pie in front of them. He pulled out a chair and joined them, but not before removing the sheriff's Stetson from the tabletop to safety on the extra seat.

"What's up?" That question came from Beau, blond and blue-eyed, the cousin who raised daylilies by the thousands and had made local history back in the summer by being featured in some magazine. "Zeni's not upset over the thing this morning, is she?"

"Frustrated probably, but not upset," Trey answered. He could have made a fine joke out of the bet, but kept it to himself. Talking about it didn't seem right, somehow. "I heard Carla made it," he went on, speaking of Beau's wife before turning to Lance. "And Mandy, too."

"Yeah, next thing we know, they'll be big stars, flying out to Hollywood."

Trey gave him a frown. "You don't mean it."

"That's his worry," Beau said in confiding tones. "He's so sure Mandy's star material, he can't help thinking she'll be enticed away from him."

"Bull," Lance told him with a frown.

"Gospel." Beau gave him a pitying look. "I know, because the same thing has passed through my mind about Carla."

Trey shook his head. "Neither of you has anything to worry about. The ladies you married are too smart to go for that phony stuff."

"You're right," Lance said with a slow nod.

"Sure, I'm right." Privately, Trey thought again that it was a good thing Zeni hadn't caught that guy Derek's eye at the morning's tryout.

"Didn't you just get back from a bike race?" Lance asked. "How did you make out?"

Trey told them, tacking on a story about the 1965 Electra Glide Harley in candy apple red with a panhead engine that some guy had been showing off as his dream ride.

"Guess one of those will be showing up in your garage with your other toys," Lance said.

"I'd rather have basic black, but yeah. It would already be there except I need to save my nickels and dimes."

"Since when?" Irony was strong in the sheriff's voice.

"Since I got the chance to buy out the shares of my other relatives in the old home place."

"Finally," Beau said, sitting back in his chair.

"Finally is right," he answered, "but it's all done, signed and sealed. It's mine."

The sheriff narrowed his eyes at him. "You're planning on living out there, are you?"

"Don't see why not."

"The front steps are falling down, for starters. Half the doors won't close, much less lock, and it's overrun with cats."

Trey had to laugh at that dire description. "Yeah, you and Mandy spent a night out there a while back, didn't you?"

"That we did."

Beau spoke up with curiosity in his voice. "This would be while the two of you were running from the goons that were after her?"

"And I was dumb enough to give her such a hard time that she tried to sleep in the old house instead of in the RV with me." Lance shook his head before turning to Trey. "The point is, you'll need to do a lot of work before you can live in the place."

"I'm on it," Trey said. In fact, he was looking forward to it, couldn't wait to get started. "If either of you two feel an urge to lend a hand, I won't mind."

They both started to nodded, which was no more than he'd expected. Before they could open their mouths, however, Gloria came to a halt at their table with her notepad in hand.

"Hey there, boss man. Zeni says you need something to sweeten your disposition. She's cutting you a big slice of lemon pie, but wants to know if you need milk or coffee with that."

Beau and Lance put their heads down, working on their own pie slices. Trey thought Beau's shoulders might be shaking with a silent laugh, but couldn't be sure. What the two of them found so entertaining about his dealings with Zeni, he didn't know, but thought it had something to do with the fact that they had both married within the last year and a half or so.

He shot a look in Zeni's direction, but her concentration was on what she was doing. Yeah, more than it had to be.

"You tell her—" he began, but stopped. "Never mind. I'll tell her."

It was then that the coffee shop door opened to admit a surge of warm air and a couple of Hollywood types, one of them the man half the town was falling over themselves to know, the actor, Derek Peabody. The man paused, as if making an obligatory entrance. The fluorescent lights over-head flashed on his sunglasses before he ripped them from his face with a flamboyant gesture and handed them to the tall blonde assistant at his side. Rapidly scanning the room, he allowed his gaze to settle on Zeni as she stood behind the counter, chef's knife upraised in her fist and her expression far from welcoming.

"*There* you are," Peabody exclaimed as if she had been lost and now he'd found her. "I told my people to see to it you stayed behind when the others had gone, but they failed me. It was necessary to discover who you were and where I might find you."

"Fine," Zeni said, not giving an inch. "May I help you?"

"Oh, yes, I should think so, sweetheart. That you are named for Zenobia, the great queen of the desert who appears in *Brief Candles*, is a marvelous omen for the movie's success. These things are meant to be."

"But I'm actually Zenia, which comes from the Greek. My mother was studying the language when she and my father met."

He waved that away with a wide gesture. "Close enough. You will be my Zenobia!"

CHAPTER THREE

"You're saying you want to give me a part?"

Zeni needed to be absolutely certain before she dared allow herself to believe it, or even glance toward where Trey stood. It was exciting if true, but her first thought was for how it might affect the bet with her boss. Some things were just more important.

"Indeed I am," Peabody answered in brisk tones. "It isn't exactly a starring role, you understand, but an important scene pivots on it."

She did look at Trey then; she couldn't help it. Here was vindication if she'd ever seen it. He didn't notice, however, but stood scowling at the movie actor with his hands closed into fists. She turned back to Peabody.

"I'm afraid I don't quite see how an ancient warrior queen like Zenobia fits into a modern comedy-drama."

He came forward, his smile shaded with surprise as he

took a seat on one of the stools at the counter. "How amazing that you realize who Zenobia was, my dear. I'm gratified, as it bodes well for the movie. But you're quite right that she would have no place. She only appears in a dream sequence. The set will be grand and mysterious, monumental, even. Picture the kind of thing done for *Cleopatra*."

Cleopatra. Right.

That particular movie was before her time and didn't end too well for the Queen of the Nile, the way Zeni remembered it. "And you're sure you want me to play Zenobia?"

"You have the striking look I want, plus that air of haughty, damn-your-eyes confidence," he said with a swirling gesture around his own face. "It will translate well before the camera, I think. I'm seldom wrong about these things."

Trey made a soft sound that might have been disbelief, but sounded more like disgust. It touched Zeni on the raw. "Well, of course," she said without taking her gaze from the actor/director, "if you're sure I'm right for the part, I'll be happy to give it a try."

"Excellent!" Peabody slapped the countertop. "You'll have to do a screen test. And it goes without saying that you'll need to change your appearance for it."

"Now wait a minute," she began.

"Not that you aren't charmingly unique, up to a point, but you realize your personality must be submerged in that of Queen Zenobia. That will require a more classic look which can then be enhanced with makeup, jewelry and costume, but we do need to see a more simplified you."

"Oh, but—"

"It will only be for the screen test, you understand. Well, and for the filming if the test goes well. Afterward, you can go back to being yourself, whatever that self may be. That's if it's what you want."

Zeni almost told him to take his part and shove it. She was happy as she was, thank you very much. More than that, she resented the implication that she might be so affected by her experience as a bit player in his film that she might never be the same.

"And of course, I will be available if you have questions." His smile turned intimate and his voice dropped to a lower register. "The two of us will be working closely on this scene—closely indeed, as I play the lead who intrudes on you, the great queen, during his dream. I would be pleased to give you my opinion on your appearance for the test."

Trey walked to the counter, looming up behind the actor. "No need for that," he said. "Zeni has friends who can tell her whatever she needs to know."

Peabody turned on the stool to give Trey a fast up and down appraisal. "You among them, I suppose?"

"Head of the line," Trey assured him.

"How very nice for her." The man stood, deliberately turning his back on Trey without bothering to give his name or ask for one. To Zeni, he said, "My assistant will take your contact information and phone later with the date and location for the screen test. She will also provide a few lines for you to learn and speak on camera. I look forward to seeing how that turns out. Until then?"

Zeni said something in reply, though she wasn't sure what. She stood with her chef's knife still upraised in front of her while she watched Peabody and his assistant sweep out the door.

The whole thing had been so surreal, and over so fast, that she wasn't totally sure it had happened. That was, until Derek Peabody was out of earshot.

Trey swore under his breath, a sound almost drowned out as Lance, Beau and the half a dozen other customers in the shop whooped and cheered.

It was true then. Everyone had heard the offer. She was in.

Zeni put down her knife. Moving in something close to slow motion, she turned to face Trey. A smile curved her mouth as she met the rain-cloud gray of his eyes.

"I won," she said in dulcet tones.

"Now, Zeni—"

"I did. I won."

He shoved his hands into the pockets of his jeans. "The bet was for getting hired as an extra, not for a bit part."

"Don't crawfish. I won fair and square, and you know it. So—about that full-body massage?"

"You're joking, right?"

She gave a slow shake of her head as she watched the hot color that crept up his neck and into his face. "And I don't have any muddy boots, but you could paint my toenails. I have this new color called Tantalizing Teal."

"I wasn't going to make you do those things, I swear," he

said, perspiration breaking out on his upper lip. "I just couldn't resist teasing a little."

"Is that what you call it?" The room was growing quieter as the hubbub died away. She couldn't spin this out much longer, nor could she embarrass him in front of his friends and neighbors, as tempting as it might be. "Then you won't mind that I did the same."

"You mean—" His expression went from panic to relief in a nanosecond. "Whew! I thought you meant it for a minute there."

She pursed her lips and laid a finger alongside her cheek. "That doesn't mean I'm forgetting you owe me. There is something you can do."

The coffee shop went quiet so suddenly it seemed it must have a mute button. Trey's eyes narrowed as he realized, as she did, that they were the focus of every eye in the place. He swallowed so hard his Adam's apple rose and fell in the strong brown column of his throat.

"And that would be?"

"You can spend a day helping me get ready for this bit part, just as you said, making me look like someone who could be Zenobia the Warrior Queen."

Trey's eyes narrowed in appraisal as they rested on her, almost as though he'd never really looked at her before. If he was aware that everyone in the coffee shop was waiting for his answer, he gave no sign. The seconds ticked past before he inclined his head in slow and considered agreement.

"Looks like I've got my work cut out for me, but—when do we start?"

Trey felt more than a little self-conscious as he stood in the living area of the apartment above the coffee shop that Zeni rented. It was the first time he'd been upstairs here since she'd moved into the space. It didn't look the same at all. In fact, it looked like Zeni, he thought, a weird mixture of the exotic, trendy, and staid.

She'd painted the walls mushroom gray—when had that happened?—and hung a collection of modern art prints with swirls and zigzags in vivid colors. A ceramic owl the size of a small dog sat on the antique mantle that was left over from when the place had been an old stage stop, while next to it was an antique French clock with spindly gilded legs topped by cherubs. A couple of giant seashells rested atop the bookcase in one corner. In front of the gray tweed sofa sat a carved camphor wood chest centered on a sisal rug, while flung over the cushions was what appeared to be a length of sari silk. If he wasn't mistaken, it had little brass bells sewn along the edge of one end.

The whole place, like the coffee shop's grill area below when Zeni was in charge, was scrupulously clean. The only thing out of place was a book lying on the chest that served as a coffee table, and the tea cup that sat beside it. She must've been up for a while, either out of habit or from being keyed up over the coming screen test.

She was usually down in the coffee shop making biscuits and frying sausage now, at four in the morning. Gloria was busy with that chore at the moment. Trey wasn't too sure why Zeni wanted to get started on her Zenobia preparation so early, but he'd promised, so here he stood.

She'd let him in, but then disappeared into the bedroom. He wasn't sure whether she intended to get dressed so they could go somewhere, or just change out of the short kimono she'd had on for a housecoat. It was all the same to him, either way, since his brain was still short-circuited by the sight of her pale thighs and elegantly shaped calves beneath the short hem as she'd walked away from him. His heart was still tapping on his ribs as if playing a xylophone.

It didn't seem right, somehow, to make himself at home by taking a seat. He wandered to the bookcase and leaned closer to check out the titles; he'd read somewhere that looking at a person's collection of books was like getting a peep into their minds, and he wouldn't mind the insight. He lifted a brow as he saw biographies, poetry, philosophy, literary and feminist classics sharing space with romances and mysteries. He didn't know why he was surprised, however; he'd figured out quite a while ago that Zeni was no dummy.

"What do you think?"

He snapped erect as Zeni spoke behind him. For a second, it was almost as if she'd read his mind. Then he saw that she held a clothes hanger in each hand, both with long evening dresses, and had a questioning look on her face.

"Well," he began, at something of a loss.

"I looked up Zenobia on the Internet, and she was shown wearing a Roman robe and cloak in one painting and a jeweled gown, a crown and lots of jewelry in another." She held up a long white dress with her right hand and a sequined number in black and gold with her left.

Trey looked from one to the other before he met her inquiring brown gaze. "Did Peabody say to show up in costume?"

"No. Why?"

"I could be wrong, but I don't think that's the way this screen test thing works. They just want to know how your face picks up the light, what its planes and angles look like through the camera lens, maybe what your voice is like. After that, it's whether you can read a few lines and make them sound natural."

"It's a bit part. I doubt I'll have much to say."

"Yeah, so it'll be mostly about your face and hair, and maybe how you move."

"And you know this how?" Suspicion was strong in her voice.

He shrugged. "I can look up things on the Internet, too."

"I don't know," she said after a moment, still studying the dresses she held. "It seems dressing the part should help."

"It's not really about the part, since they can work on that later. It's about how you come across on film."

She sighed, and then stepped to the sofa, throwing the two dresses across the arm. "Fine, if you say so." She dusted her hands as if done with one idea and ready for the next. "Where do we start on that?"

Trey knew better than to answer in words; it would just get him in trouble. Folding his arms over his chest, he cocked his head to one side and studied Zeni with care, studied her for the pleasure of it. He already knew what he wanted to do, since he'd thought of little else for several hours during the night just past.

"Trey—" Nervousness and irritation were strong in her voice.

"Shh. I'm thinking."

"Well, don't take too long, or I'm going to tell Derek Peabody to forget the whole thing!"

She would, too; Trey didn't doubt it for a second. She was already fidgeting, stacking one bare foot over the other while pulling the ends of her kimono sash so it tightened at her narrow waist, giving her a shape to make a man drool. Still, he waited another two seconds before he started moving toward her.

She blinked and backed up a step. Was it something she saw in his face, or just a natural reaction to his slow prowl?

It didn't matter. He put out a hand to catch her right fist, unwrapping her fingers from her kimono sash. Holding it with care, he reached to touch the ring in her nose.

"Wait a minute!" she exclaimed as he turned the nasal adornment with gentle and easy moves until the catch was uppermost. "What are you doing?"

"You think Zenobia had one of these?"

"She may have." The words were defensive. She pulled her head back, away from his hand.

"Doubtful. She was from the ancient Palmyra in what is now Iraq, not India."

"How do you—I suppose you read up on that as well."

"I had to, didn't I? To be sure I wouldn't tell you something wrong."

"It's wrong if I don't want to give up my nose ring!" She declared in waspish protest.

"And why would you want to keep it? In India, it can be a sign a woman is married."

She was still for an instant. "Really?"

"Really. You haven't been married, have you?" He paused to take in her fulminating stare. "No, I didn't think so."

"It doesn't matter. I don't have to be Indian to like the style."

"Do you like it, or is it a way to thumb your nose, literally, at society and all the folks who don't have holes in their noses?"

"What a thing to say!"

"Even if you love it, you have to worry about whether you'll get the part while it's in place, right? That is if you really want a chance at this bit of playacting?"

"Of course I want it."

The words were firm, but Trey wasn't sure he believed her. She didn't meet his eyes, for one thing. For another, she seemed not to realize that he'd unfastened her nose ring and was slowly sliding it from its mooring.

It was simple enough; a quick flick of his thumbnail and the ring flew open. A few small movements, and the uppermost curved ring section slowly glided from that tiny opening in her body. It was such a sensual move that he was tempted to reverse the act, sliding it back into the hole.

Suddenly it was free. He held it, warm from her body, in his hand. Slowly, he closed his fist upon it as if in holding it, he held a piece of her.

Jeez, he needed to get a grip. If he didn't watch out, he'd get himself thrown out of her apartment on his ear.

She switched her gaze to his, her own dark. "Fine, then. No nose ring. Is that all?"

It was a challenge. She was daring him to continue along the path he'd started. He drew a deep breath and let it out again. "Next thing is your hair."

"My hair."

"You did ask for my help," he reminded her.

Thought flickered behind the mirrors of her eyes before she frowned. "I could wear a wig."

"Too uncomfortable," he said at once. "Especially if you get the part and then have to spend a week or so filming."

"It can't take that long," she protested.

"You never know. If you're really good—" He let that trail away as if contemplating the prospect, and maybe the future that lay before her.

"Ridiculous," she said with a ladylike snort. "I'll probably just be some figure barely seen through swirling purple smoke or some such thing."

"Maybe, and maybe not." He grinned. "But if you are, I don't think you want your hair to match the smoke."

The frustration on her face told him he had her.

"I guess you think I should color it some natural color," she said through semi-clenched teeth.

"If you can remember what your natural shade might

be," he said in agreement. With a negligent, almost reflex action, he slid the nose ring he held into his pants pocket.

"I remember, thank you very much."

"Dark brown, almost black?" It was a guess, made as he took his hand from his pocket again, though he really wanted to know. Why, he wasn't sure.

"Medium brown."

"Good. Try for that," he said in mild suggestion, rather than as any kind of order. "It's probably close to the real Zenobia's natural color, anyway."

She gave him a suspicious stare. "Not coal black hair?"

"Could be, but those old sheikhs collected their wives and harem women from all over Eastern Europe as well as the Middle East and the Orient. Auburn and blonde looks were highly prized."

"But not purple, I suppose."

He chuckled, as much in appreciation for her resigned attempt at humor as for what she'd said. "Not so much."

"Got it. No costume, no nose ring, natural hair color. Anything else?"

"Minimal eye makeup and none of those red squiggles." She sighed. "Henna designs."

"And no apron," he went on, his face solemn.

"No tank top, either, I suppose?"

"Not likely. What do you have instead?"

"You want to check out my wardrobe?" The question had an extra long-suffering sound.

No, he didn't. "Maybe."

Trey wasn't sure why he was doing this. He didn't want

Zeni to be in the movie, didn't want her mixed up with Peabody and maybe becoming another one of his groupies. He didn't want her associating with the leading man at all, now that he'd met the guy. Nor did he want her too close to the whole movie crowd with their lax attitudes and predatory habits. Zeni wasn't exactly an innocent, he was sure, but she was no match for the kind of amoral goings-on that turned up so often in the gutter press.

So why in hell was he here?

Because it was something Zeni wanted, something that had meaning for her, one way or another. Because he'd made a bet, and he honored his debts.

"In here," Zeni said shortly, and led the way into her bedroom. Walking to her narrow closet, she pushed open its sliding door and stepped back.

Trey had seen women's closets before. He had two sisters, both of whom were married and living out of state, and he'd also lived with a couple of females at different times. Compared to past experience, there was next to nothing on the rack in Zeni's closet. The items were grouped into categories and had at least an inch of space between each one. Six tanks tops in different colors, four T-shirts, one long-sleeved white dress shirt, an extra jean skirt, two pairs of jeans, and one pair of black dress slacks was the total count. On the floor underneath was one pair each of running shoes, brown leather sandals and black heels. That was the sum total.

His brows climbed his forehead. He'd thought he had seen her in more outfits. The difference was apparently in the wild assortment of belts and scarves, silk and velvet flowers, lace and net shawls and chains and beads that hung on the back of the closet door. "This is all?"

"It's enough."

"But the two dresses you showed me. Where did they—"

"Thrift store."

"I hope you can get your money back," he muttered, only half to himself.

"No problem. And so?" She leaned a shoulder against the door's frame, crossing her arms over her chest.

The move lifted her breasts under the silk of her short housecoat, making it clear she wore no bra under it. Trey had to look deep into the closet and clear his throat before he could form an answer. "I say wear the gray tank top under the white shirt and with the black slacks."

"No color and maybe the heels for a French vibe?" she asked with sardonic amusement in her voice.

"That's it."

"I think I could have figured that out, once the costume idea was out of the picture."

"Yeah," he answered, frowning again at the scarcity of choices for her. It also crossed his mind that knowledge of the most sophisticated ensemble choice from what was available didn't exactly go with what he thought of as Zeni's style. What else was he missing about her?

She pushed away from the door facing. "Now that's settled, would you like coffee?"

"If you have it already made."

"I can put some on. It will be ready in just a minute."

"No, that's okay."

She paused halfway out of the room, glancing at him over her shoulder with one lifted brow.

Trey shook his head. "You were having tea, I think. That's fine for me, too." The idea was to save her the trouble of doing something extra.

"Hot tea? You?"

"It's been known to happen."

Her smile was crooked before she walked away. "I'll put some ice in it for you."

"Good," he said under his breath as he swiped a hand across his forehead while watching her regal carriage that didn't quite disguise the sway of her hips. "Ice will be really good."

CHAPTER FOUR

*T*rey's advice not only toned down her personality and style, but almost neutralized it. Zeni wasn't sure he meant it that way, but the effect was the same.

Maybe it was necessary to get the part, and maybe not. There wasn't much use complaining, however, since she'd asked for it.

She might have guessed how it would turn out. Maybe she had; maybe she'd wanted to see how he'd change her if he could—or if he'd change her at all.

If so, she had her answer.

Nothing about it was permanent, of course. When this movie deal was done, she could go back to being her true self, just as Derek Peabody had said. That was, if she could figure out exactly what that might look like. She wasn't totally sure, hadn't been for a long time.

"That's the way," Trey said as he followed behind her into the kitchen. "Exactly like that!"

She glanced at him over her shoulder with suspicion as she took down a glass from the cabinet, poured warm tea from her old blue teapot into it. "What's the way?"

"That walk with your chin up, nose in the air and shoulders straight, as if you're queen of all you survey and the rest of us are mere peasants."

"I don't do that!" She found a spoon and stirred sugar into the tea, the metal hitting the sides of a glass with an agitated tinkling.

"Sure you do, every time you get mad at me and go stalking off." His eyes were silvery with amusement as he watched her put his glass under the refrigerator's ice dispenser.

"Remembering it should be no problem then. All I have to do is think of you at your most annoying."

"Yeah, I expect that'll do it," he answered, his smile fading.

Her fingers touched his as she handed him the tea. The zing of it along her nerve endings was almost painful. It was also more natural and familiar than she wanted to admit, after the months she'd been around him. That the reaction never seemed to go away was the strange part.

It was also unusual for them to be alone like this, just the two of them. Their sparring was a public sport, complete with customers for referees if things got out of hand. Not that they ever did; Trey saw to that. He was the one who walked away when things threatened to escalate to the point

TRISTAN ON A HARLEY | 51

where she was going to quit or get herself fired. She'd like to think that was because he didn't want her to go, but was all too aware it could be he didn't want to have to find a replacement.

"All right, then. You've fixed my jewelry, my clothes and the way I walk. Besides, my hair, what's left?"

He watched her for long moments. "Does it bother you? I mean, really? I'm not criticizing, just trying to help out the way you asked."

"I know." She stepped into the living room to retrieve her tea cup, bringing it back to reheat in the microwave for a few seconds.

"What I'm trying to say is, you're just fine at the Watering Hole. It's this movie thing that makes it different. If you were trying out for a comedy part, your hair color and so on would be okay."

Her smile was wry. "You'd better stop while you're ahead."

"Maybe I had, at that," he said, looking away, though his face cleared after a second. "So, are you going to model the outfit for me that you'll be wearing?"

"I don't think so." The answer was automatic, with no thought whatever.

"Too boring for you?"

"Too satisfying for you." Irony still lingered in her smile. "Besides, you'll see it at the screen test."

"Who said I was going to be there?"

She gave him an inquiring look. "Aren't you? Out of curiosity at the very least?"

The look on his face said he hadn't considered it. That was hardly a surprise, since he had zero interest in what was going on. Chamelot might be slowly turning movie mad, but that wasn't Trey. He liked things real, not artificial.

Zeni frowned at that thought. She knew that about him, had known it from the first time she met him, when she walked into the Watering Hole and asked for a job. Was it, just possibly, the reason she'd become more out there with her hair and makeup every passing week? Protective coloration, as it were? A way to make sure she didn't appeal to him, so she—

What? Wouldn't have to deal with it if he decided to come on to her? Or needn't feel bad if he ignored any opportunity?

She didn't want or need entanglements. She was single and proud of it. She'd been on her own for years and preferred it that way.

Zeni had never been part of a big family. The closest she'd come was her association with the Benedicts these past couple of years, Trey's cousins, Lance and Beau, and their wives. There were advantages in that: she didn't have a lot of birthdays and anniversaries to remember, didn't have to cook for family gatherings or decide where she was going for Thanksgiving or Christmas.

Of course, nobody knew or remembered her birthday, and she celebrated the holidays alone.

She liked it like that, most of the time. She also liked it when someone added her to their family gathering.

"You want me to show up?" Trey asked.

It was an instant before she could form an answer; she'd almost forgotten what they were talking about. To answer with another question seemed better than saying she didn't much want to go through her screen test alone.

"Don't you want to see your handiwork?"

He studied her a moment, his eyes unnaturally grave. It almost seemed he could see right through her. And wasn't that a scary thought?

"Nah," he said finally. "You'll be fine on your own."

It was better this way, she realized. If she failed, he wouldn't be there to see her do it.

"So now what? " She summoned a smile. "We still have a lot of day left. Any other pointers for making me look like a warrior queen?"

"You'll need to be bold, almost challenging. You should look people in the eye and dare them to be less than respectful toward you."

A frown pleated her brows. "I thought I did that."

"Sometimes. Other times you back off as if you want to disappear."

He was entirely too perceptive. Yes, and when she least expected it.

"No such thing!"

"No?"

The sympathy in his eyes was almost her undoing. For one thing, he looked far too dewy-eyed-handsome with understanding in his face. Then she also didn't want him feeling sorry for her. She was fine, had been fine since coming to Chamelot, escaping the pigeonhole she'd been rattling around in since she started to school, that of being too smart for her own good. She'd abandoned her nerdy image along with the triple degrees in mathematics, English literature and environmental chemistry, all earned before she was eighteen. Dumbing down from her stratospheric IQ so she could fit in, avoiding big words and complicated ideas had been a small price to pay for acceptance. She'd been happy enough, hiding out behind her borderline outré image so no one could get close enough to question that camouflage for her brainpower. Being singled out now felt like something she should have avoided.

The only trouble was that another part of her was gladdened by the special attention. And wasn't that a sad thing to realize?

"Oh, well," she said with as much nonchalance as she could manage. "We are all weird, each in our own way. So what do you suggest I do to look more queenly?"

"If I remember the bet right, we have a whole day to work on it," Trey paused for an instant. "Want to take a bike ride?"

Zeni didn't care for bikes, especially the big Harley Davidson motorcycles Trey favored. Their high speed and lack of protection for the rider; their weaving progress through traffic and exposure to sun, wind, rain and bug assaults all seemed like willful testing of disaster. Riding one was bad enough, but clinging to the back of someone, with no control of the situation, struck her as the height of foolishness, if not proof of a joint suicide pact.

Yet she envied Trey when he took off from the coffee

shop on his Harley, swaying in and out of the slow traffic on Main Street with masculine grace, sublimely free and unfettered, completely without care.

"Sure," she said. "Why not?"

She wore jeans as covering for the bare skin of her legs, just in case they had an accident. Her T-shirt had much the same purpose, though she wished it had long sleeves. And the pair of old-fashioned goggles she slapped on over her eyes was something more than a fashion accessory.

She clung to Trey with both arms clamped around his waist, her cheek pressed to his broad back for the protection against flies, gnats and moths. But it was also a fine excuse to be close to his hard strength, to feel the subtle vibration of the machine underneath them as it coursed through his muscles and sinews and then into her own. And if their swift, windswept passage, racing their shadow over the pavement, had an element of almost orgasmic excitement, that was her secret.

They swerved from the main road after a bit, taking a dirt track. The trees overhead created a cool green tunnel, one which they rode through like a surfer threading a turquoise ocean pipe. Dust billowed out behind them, cream and rust from the mix of sands, though they outrode it all the way to what appeared to be a driveway. It billowed past them as they turned again, coating the road's edging of dried grass and the nodding weeds with a fine powder.

The house appeared at the end of the drive. It was large and imposing, yet oddly human in scale, another of the many old plantation houses that dotted the area. Trees, vines and head-high shrubs had taken possession of what had once been farmland behind it. They encroached on the house as well, with honeysuckle and saw briers climbing the shutters, and massive azaleas doing their best to cover the front steps.

It was a Southern Planter's Cottage in style, with one main floor and a second one under the steep roof that received light through dormer windows. The floor-to-ceiling windows across the front were protected by shutters, as was the fan-lighted entrance door, and all were set behind a long, railed porch. The building appeared almost derelict, however, fighting a desperate rearguard action against the forces of nature that were trying to take it down.

Trey eased the bike to a stop and put out his feet to brace it on either side. For long moments, he simply sat looking at the place.

"This is where Lance and Mandy hid out for a day or two last year, isn't it, when those mafia guys were after her?" Zeni scooted from behind him, dismounting as she removed her helmet and dropped her goggles inside it.

He tipped his head in a nod. "They pulled the RV out of sight around the back. I've never seen a female as happy as Mandy was when she saw the clothes you sent her."

"Being half naked while in the company of a man you don't know from Adam can do that to a woman." Her voice held more than a little asperity.

"Guess I'll never be able to check that out," he said and heaved a sigh.

"I should hope not, if it includes people trying to kill

you."

He gave her a quick grin as he removed his helmet, then took hers and hung both on the handlebars, but he made no answer.

A sidewalk of faded red brick led toward the house's front steps. Zeni followed it, scuffling through mats of decaying leaves, avoiding patches of green moss, stepping over rotted limbs and twigs. The motorcycle's engine rumbled to a stop behind her as Trey turned the key, and she heard his footsteps when he trailed after her. His progress was stop-and-go, however, as if he was assessing the place for future reference.

"So what's this about?" she asked over her shoulder. "You feeling a sudden yen to get back to your roots?"

"Something like that."

She'd been kidding, just getting in a dig at him as she'd done a thousand times before. Something in his voice as he answered snagged her attention. She halted and turned back toward him.

"Really? You mean it?"

"I own the place now. Several relatives were involved in the ownership after my granddad died. My dad signed over his interest to me, and I finally raised enough money to buy out my sisters and a couple of aunts and uncles."

"And you're going to do what with it? Spend a fortune restoring this big barn of a house and then live in it?"

"Is that so hard to believe?"

An acid retort crossed her mind, but the defensive sound of his voice kept her from letting fly with it. He expected her to be scathing, and that made her wary. It was an odd turn of affairs.

"It will take a lot of work," she said instead, turning back to stare at the house.

"Or a good contractor, after I get some of the clean-up done." He stopped beside her.

She tilted her head. "I'm pretty good with a broom."

"You mean it?" The look he directed toward her was more than a little surprised.

She did, oddly enough. Something about the mats of leaves on the steps leading up to the porch, the layer of dirt scum on its floor and the grime on the old wavy glass of the one or two windows uncovered by shutters made her itch to get to work. It had nothing to do with Trey, however. No, not at all. It was only that she hated dirt and disorder on general principles.

"Why not?" she asked with a challenge in her eyes, daring him to make something of it.

Why not, indeed, Trey thought, as he gazed down at Zeni.

It was a novel experience, being of the same mind with her. Though they saw each other nearly every day, she was usually so busy or prickly that they never really connected. Oh, they discussed the day-to-day running of his different enterprises, but they were brief exchanges, all business. To talk to her, be close to her, provide something that gained her interest, was an event worth extending.

Besides, they had just arrived, and he wasn't ready to head back to town and all his usual responsibilities, much less the sight and sound of the movie company invasion.

"The problem," he said deliberately, as he turned back to survey his property, "is figuring out where to start."

"Right here and right now is always a good answer," Zeni said, and gave him a smile that set the blood to sizzling in his veins.

An hour later, the leaves were gone from the steps, and the porch—the part of it not so rotten it was dangerous to set foot on it—was clear of vines and bits of limbs and engrained dirt. This was all done with a rusty knife found in the barn out back and a piece of a broom discovered in the closet under the stairs. Though it was a pleasant fall day, they were both hot, sweaty, and in need of something cold to drink by the time they had made a showing.

Trey pulled a couple of bottles of water from the insulated bag attached to the bike. Handing one to Zeni, he pulled off his T-shirt over his head and used it to wipe the sweat from his face and the back of his neck before settling beside her. He dropped the T-shirt between them, and then twisted the cap from his water.

"You missed a scratch," she said. Picking up the shirt, she dabbed at a place on his face. It stung a bit, and the shirt came away with a smear of red.

He jerked his head back in surprise. "Saw brier must have got me."

It was the best Trey could do since his brain was muddled by sudden, frying heat as she leaned close enough for him to catch her fresh yet exotic scent. It was compounded of sweet peas and patchouli, he knew, since he'd seen the bottle in her bedroom, but was enhanced a hundred times over by its grace note of warm woman.

"You need to put something on it when we get back."

He didn't need her to tell him that, but appreciated the thought, anyway.

They drank their water in silence, while a breeze cooled their skin and sent dried leaves drifting down from the trees that surrounded the house, bringing with it the scents of parched grass, goldenrod and ripe muscadine grapes. The distant cawing of crows and high-pitched cry of a hawk added to the serenity of the Indian summer.

Just then, a mewling sound came from the tall grass that grew at the edge of the trees. As they glanced in that direction, a small black cat stepped daintily around a clump of sedge and sat down, curling his tail around his feet as he watched them. He looked interested but wary.

That a cat was somewhere around was no great surprise; the house smelled of them, and there was evidence they made their home on a stack of old blankets in an upstairs bedroom. Trey knew they hung close, but had made no attempt to remove them. They paid for their shelter by keeping down the rat population. Besides, he'd played with their ancestors when he was a kid.

"It's a kitten," Zeni said, her voice hushed.

"And probably feral," he said by way of agreement.

"Where on earth did it come from?"

"My grandmother used to feed a dozen or more barn

cats when she was alive, but it's been a while. They've mostly gone back to the wild. I bring a sack or two of cat food when I come out here, but only catch a glimpse of one now and then."

Zeni held out her hand toward the little feline, calling quietly, "Here kitty, kitty."

"I doubt it will come." It wasn't that he was the pessimist she'd called him. He just hated to see her try her wiles for nothing.

"He doesn't look wild," she said with confidence.

"I wouldn't try to catch him. You'd probably get scratched worse than I did from the saw briers."

"I think he's lonesome and wants company."

She called again, her voice so low and enticing that Trey could feel the sound invading his senses, gaining strength on its way down his body to the crotch of his jeans. If she ever called him like that, he thought in wry humor, he'd be all over her.

The kitten must have felt the same. It rose and glided into a walk, making a semi-circle around her from one direction, and then reversing, coming just a bit nearer with the second pass.

"Here, little kitty," Zeni called in soft seduction. "I'll scratch your ears for you and rub your back. You can even sit on my lap, if you like."

A corner of Trey's mouth tug upward in a wry grin as his back began to itch. The power of suggestion, he was sure, wishing she'd scratch his back, but a fine daydream all the same.

A second later, he was forced to sit and watch as the feline stretched out its neck to sniff Zeni's fingers, and then give them a swift lick. Slowly, but with every sign of pleasurable domesticity, it began to weave back and forth across her ankles. When she reached down with slow care and picked it up, the kitten gave a meow of surprise but didn't fight her. Seconds later, it was sitting on her lap, getting its ears scratched.

"I'll be damned," he said.

Her fingers were gentle but sure, and a small smile curved her lips as she ran her hand over the cat's glossy fur. She hesitated, and then gave Trey a quick glance from under her lashes.

"Do you suppose I could have him?"

He stared at her in frank surprise. "You want to keep it?"

"I never had a cat growing up. My mom was allergic to them."

"He probably has fleas."

"I can give him a bath, maybe take him to the vet for shots," she answered, a pleading noted in her voice he was sure was unintentional. "He's yours, isn't he, if he lives here? And you own the apartment above the coffee shop. You get to decide."

He hadn't thought about that; still he shrugged. "It's all right with me, as long as he doesn't wander around downstairs. I think there are laws against cats in food places. Dogs, too, of course, unless they're service animals."

"Deal," she said, as she scratched behind the kitten's ears. "Midnight will be a good boy, won't you?"

"You've named him already? Sure of yourself, aren't you?"

"You said I should be bolder," she answered with a spark of laughter in her eyes as she looked up at him. "Guess you were right."

What could he say to that? He watched her pet the cat while long seconds slid past. "You don't mind that he's black?"

"Should I?" Her gaze was curious and somehow wary, as if she thought he intended to rescind his permission.

"Some people think they're unlucky. They deliberately run over them if they see them crossing the road in front of them."

"Superstitious idiots."

He had to agree, since he'd never seen that color made a bit of difference to the nature of the cats his grandmother kept all her life. Or to that of the human race, when it came right down to it.

The only sound for a few minutes was the soft rumbling of the cat's purr. It was a peaceful sound, adding to the odd contentment of the day. That was until Zeni looked up, her expression guarded, as if she was suddenly wary of the companionship growing between them.

With a nod toward the house behind them, she said, "I guess all the antique furnishings in there are yours, too?"

"They are, though what you saw are mostly the things too heavy to be moved. I packed up the rest and put it in storage."

"Super."

"There are a few good pieces, yeah. I meant to bring a camera to take photos for insurance appraisal, but forgot it."

"I meant super that you won't have to buy everything new."

He inclined his head. "Some folks would toss out most of it in favor of modern stuff with light woods and clean lines. I like the old things, and figure they'll be back in style one day. Then everybody will be throwing out the minimalist stuff they're buying now."

"You may be right," she said on a quick laugh.

"What about you? You like old and fancy, or does it have to be new and simple?"

"I don't know. I've only ever had old and simple." She ran her hand down the kitten's back and then brushed away a puffball of fur.

"No family heirlooms at your grandparent's house?"

"No grandparents."

"None?" He couldn't keep the doubt out of his voice.

"Well, none that I ever knew. Or ever wanted to, really."

"How did that happen?"

She didn't answer for the space of several breaths, long enough that Trey thought she was going to refuse.

Finally she made a brief gesture with one hand. "My mother's parents were both doctors, a surgeon and an obstetrician. When my mom got pregnant at seventeen, they pressured her to have an abortion, told her she was stupid for not taking advantage of the arrangements they could make. She left home before they could insist on the procedure."

"With the baby's father?"

"I don't know—she never said. There was no marriage that I know of, and no man I ever called daddy. That means no grandparents on the paternal side, either." Zeni's smile was brief. A leaf floated down, landing on top of her foot. She picked it up and began to shred it.

It was obvious she was uncomfortable talking about her family. Trey could respect that. He searched his mind for a different subject, but only came up with one thing.

"Getting back to the furniture, you'd maybe keep the best things then add a few pieces that are—different, the way you did in your apartment?"

"I guess."

"That's what I figured on doing, though I'm not much of a decorator. He summoned a disarming grin as he saw the consideration in the gaze she turned on him. "I do like the color you painted the apartment walls, that sort of grey-tan, or whatever you call it. Maybe you can pick out paint chips for me when the time comes."

"Sure. Why not?"

Trey thought he might have overdone the nonchalant bit as she looked away, her face turning bleak. Yet she went on in a slightly different vein after a moment.

"You really care about this old house and all its antiques, don't you?"

"It holds a lot of memories. My granddad and grand-mamma were married in what used to be the rose garden, as were my mom and dad. A great-uncle or two went to war from here, and never came back. My granddad was a brother to Lance and Beau's grandfather, and we boys all used to come spend a month or so with him and my grandmamma every summer. She fed us her special coconut and pineapple layer cake, and he let us cut a couple of his prize watermelons and ride his old mule. We picked peaches and blackberries, nearly broke our necks jumping out of the hayloft, and half-drowned each other swimming away from water snakes in the creek that runs back behind the house."

"Fun times," she said drily.

"They were," he agreed without hesitation. "We went barefoot all day, every day, had such tough skin on the soles of our feet that we never noticed when we got thorns in them—until my grandmother decided to dig them out with a needle."

"I'd like to have seen that!"

Zeni's laugh that went along with the comment had a free-flowing sound that was good to hear. It was a moment before Trey realized her attention had wandered to his bare shoulder where a sleeve-type tattoo covered the top and swirled down his bicep, one featuring a collection of roses with thorns.

"Speaking of needles, what's this about?" she asked, her gaze shielded by her lashes as she lifted a hand and traced the rose design with a single fingertip. "Anything in particular?"

"You really want to know?" The words were deeper and slower than he'd intended, in no small part to keep his voice even in spite of the shiver that moved over him at her touch.

"If you don't mind."

"I'll tell you the story of mine if you'll tell me yours." He leaned backward a bit to glance at the top of her shoulders just below her neck. Unlike the tank tops she usually wore, her T-shirt covered the design done in sepia ink. It didn't matter. He'd memorized the dandelion seed heads with their dancing, windblown puffs, and the writing beneath that said *The answer is blowin' in the wind.*

She let her hand drop. "I don't have a story. I just like the old Bob Dylan song."

"Sure you do," he said, recognizing that for another evasion. "And I just like roses."

"Black roses with thorns? I've always heard that stands for death and pain."

He met her gaze for long seconds before looking away. "Or not."

She sighed, a soft sound of defeat. "Fine, then. My tat is because of my mother. She was bright and talented, a free soul long after the hippie generation, one who lived for the day at hand, brought me up the best way she knew how, and then died young. But I never knew what she wanted, and I'm not sure she did either."

"Figures," he said with a slow nod.

"What does that mean?"

"Only that you're a lot like that."

Outraged color bloomed across her cheekbones. "I am not!"

"No? You're on board with the Boho trends, but are almost OCD about having everything clean and in its place."

"Don't be ridiculous."

Trey watched the hauteur that bloomed in her face with satisfaction. "There, that's it. That's your Zenobia expression."

"What?"

"The look that crosses your face sometimes, a combination of superior intellect and mental withdrawal."

She drew back to stare at him. "Who, me?"

"You," he assured her with a firm nod. "Give Peabody that one during this test of yours, and the part of the warrior queen will be in the bag."

"Maybe I don't want it in the bag," she said under her breath, looking away over his shoulder while something like embarrassment spread across her features.

"Sure you do. It'll be a blast." Why he was trying to convince her when it was the last thing he wanted, Trey didn't know, except she seemed so cautious about it in some peculiar fashion.

"Maybe."

"Now tell me I'm wrong about the OCD business, too."

"Never mind. Let's hear what your tat's all about so I can psychoanalyze you."

She didn't want to talk about herself anymore; that much was clear. Not that he blamed her.

"I'm not sure you'll believe it now," he said with the twitch of his tattooed shoulder.

"And why is that?"

"Because mine's also about my mom, though she's very much alive, so no death or pain is involved. She grows roses, though, the old fashioned kind that still smell like roses should. And she loves romance novels, both new and old ones. A favorite quote of hers is from Anne Brontë, 'But he that dares not grasp the thorn should never crave the rose'."

"But that's—"

He waited, his breath caught in his chest, for her to say something sharp and derogatory. He could feel the heat of annoyance rising up the back of his neck in preparation for it.

She blinked, closed her mouth, and then opened it again. "In other words, a person afraid of getting hurt should never dream big."

"Something of that sort," he said evenly.

"That's awesome," she said with a smile of blinding brightness. "I like it."

Had she taken the quote to heart for her try-out as the warrior queen? Trey didn't know, but one thing was for sure: he didn't much like the idea that he might have clinched it for her.

CHAPTER FIVE

*T*rey had not said exactly why he wanted to restore his grandparent's old house. Was it simply a matter of family pride and tradition, or a financial move? Or did he have something else in mind?

Such as getting married?

The thought plagued Zeni as she dressed for her screen test a couple of mornings later, adding to the sick feeling in the pit of her stomach. A wife for Trey would change everything. She'd have to be careful what she said, how she acted, maybe even what she wore. Few women would appreciate the odd relationship the two of them shared, much less tolerate it. There would be no more outings to the old house he was restoring, and wouldn't that be a shame?

She hadn't noticed him with any particular female in recent weeks. Oh, he dated now and then, but it never seemed serious. When she'd first come to work at the Watering Hole, he'd had a live-in girlfriend, but that hadn't lasted. One day the woman was there, and the next she was gone.

Not that her own love life was any better, Zeni had to admit. She hadn't been serious about a man in her life since she got to Chamelot. Oh, she talked to those who came into the Watering Hole, flirted a little and enjoyed the attention, but couldn't drum up any great interest. She's been too busy settling in, getting to know her job, arranging her apartment and generally taking care of things.

Now she didn't know if she could handle it if another woman commandeered Trey's time or tried to take over at the Watering Hole. She'd have to leave, more than likely, though it was the last thing she wanted.

Zeni liked Chamelot and the people who lived there, enjoyed knowing nearly every person who walked through the door. She had almost begun to feel that she belonged. She also liked working with Trey, liked knowing that she was furthering his business interest and that he depended on her. That was all there was to it, of course; there was nothing personal in her outlook. She didn't do personal.

Yes, and though she didn't mind making his appointments and paying his business bills when he was out of town, she resented being a stand-in for his future bride. What was he thinking, having her help decide the furniture and paint colors in the home he would share with another woman?

Zeni donned the black slacks and white shirt Trey had

recommended for the screen test, but couldn't resist adding a long and dramatic necklace of bright red Murano glass beads. She'd spent several hours shampooing the semi-permanent color of her latest embellishment from her hair, and was reasonably satisfied it was now close to her glossy natural brown. When almost ready, she held her big hoop earrings up to her ears and turned her head this way and that.

No. They didn't go with her classic look. Too bad. She could have used something to boost her morale. Putting them away, she picked up her shoulder bag and headed out of the apartment.

It didn't hurt that she was met by whistles and calls of encouragement as she passed through the Watering Hole below. It was a mystery how everyone knew where she was going, but their approval helped calm the butterflies inside her.

The fairgrounds where the movie people had set up shop was a scene of controlled chaos. Equipment trucks were parked in a long row, forming a barricade between the area and the town. Their thick electrical supply lines snaked everywhere like black umbilical cords. Engines rumbled, generators hummed, and golf carts raced here and there, raising clouds of dust that hung in the air. Three motor homes and a couple of trailers were parked far enough away from the hubbub for a promise of quiet, though it was doubtful such a thing was delivered. From the largest of the permanent exhibit buildings came the aroma of fresh-brewed coffee and morning muffins and doughnuts courtesy of the Watering Hole and Trey's early morning delivery. People came and went, scattered over the acreage like an army of automatons.

Some distance back from the general melee was the old rodeo arena and the area designated for the town's medieval fair. From what Zeni had heard the evening before, the organizers were none too pleased at the preempting of their usual spot at the head of the fairgrounds. The lady mayor had done her best to mollify them, so it was said, but even the promise of having selected fair events highlighted in the movie wasn't enough to quiet the grumbling. Future publicity was no match for present inconvenience.

Zeni had no idea where she was supposed to go, but was finally directed to the main exhibit hall. As she gave her name, the woman behind the reception desk inside the door, overweight and with flyaway hair and bad skin, glared up at her.

"Where have you been?" she demanded. "You were supposed to be at makeup fifteen minutes ago."

"And I would have been, if anyone had taken the time to tell me," Zeni answered, channeling Zenobia's imperious attitude.

There was no relenting in the woman's round face. "Go now. They're waiting for you."

"Where might makeup be, if it isn't too much to ask?"

The woman waved one heavy arm. "Over there. Can't you see?"

What Zeni saw was a trailer with a miniscule sign that

did, indeed, identify it as the makeup station on close inspection. "You're too kind," she said in dry tones, before turning and striding in that direction. If there was one thing she'd learned from her mother, it was the coals-of-fire brand of extreme politeness.

She could feel the eyes of the receptionist burning into her back as she walked. The further she moved away from her, the more she regretted her retaliation. It must be difficult, dealing all day long with self-absorbed actors and other movie types, people who were more attractive than normal—good hair, good features, and good body shape— through nothing more than blind luck in the genetic sweepstakes.

Not that Zeni counted herself among them; she was okay but not exactly a raving beauty. Her eyes were a bit too big, her nose tip-tilted instead of straight, and her figure less than perfectly symmetrical—it was more like an hour glass, in fact. Altogether, it was imperfect enough that she could understand the receptionist with the cranky attitude.

The makeup artist was competent, though a bit like a butterfly, flicking sponges and brushes over Zeni's face with a light touch, flitting back and forth between her features and his makeup tray that had seen better days. It was difficult for her to sit still while he removed everything she had applied so carefully before leaving the apartment, replacing it with a far heavier layer. Noticing the signs of nervous stress in her face, he set up a calming chatter about past celebrities he'd had in his chair, his partner who was coming out from L.A. to visit, Derek's habit of yelling at people, and the role of his personal assistant who seemed to have a uniquely personal place in his life as well as having been a co-star in his Western series.

When he finally revealed her new look in his mirror, with the greater depth and more exotic tilt to her eyes, as well as higher cheekbones and her mouth done in five luscious lipstick shades, she was impressed. Even more remarkable and appreciated was that he took the time from his schedule to walk her over to where the tests for smaller parts were being filmed, giving her a word of encouragement and a quick hug before leaving her at the door.

"Zeni, honey!"

That call came from Granny Chauvin. White-haired, petite, bright-eyed and younger than her ninety-something years, she was waving with both hands. "Come here and sit by me. I heard you were up for a nice little part in this here movie. And so am I! Can you believe it?"

Zeni would have been delighted to see anyone she knew, but Granny was one of her favorite people in town, maybe in the world. She might have known she would be here, Zeni told herself as she moved toward her. She was always involved up to her sweet little neck in anything that went on in Chamelot.

"What are you here for?" she asked, dropping onto the seat of the metal folding chair beside Granny, one of several lined up in the darkened end of the building, facing what appeared to be a makeshift set.

"Nothing exciting, just playing the grandmother of the bride, or maybe great-grandmother, in some kind of wedding scene. All I have to do is walk down the aisle in a fancy dress, holding onto the arm of a handsome young man acting as an usher—no hardship, I promise you! Then I sit in the church pew looking solemn, like I've done for a bazillion real weddings."

Zeni gave her a droll look. "For this you need a screen test?"

"Oh, no, dear. I'm just here to see what's going on!" She said on a chuckle, her face pink with pleasure. "But I see you're all made up. What are you about to do?"

"A test for a dream sequence, or so I was told. I suppose they want to know if words will come out when I open my mouth. I can't imagine I'll really need to act."

"And you're far too level-headed to make this deal into something it's not, unlike some I could name." Granny nodded in the direction of a group of teens who sat giggling and chattering in breathless excitement, when they weren't tapping their thumbs on their cell phones. "It's all in good fun, not a major step to stardom."

"It might be good fun," Zeni said, "if it weren't so nerve-wracking."

"Now, never you mind." Granny reached to pat her hands that were clamped on the shoulder bag she'd placed in her lap. "You'll be just fine. All you have to do is be your own sweet self."

If Granny thought she was sweet, she must be the only one, Zeni thought in wry self-knowledge. Still, she smiled her appreciation for the thought.

"Yes, and I can't tell you how glad I am to see that nose

ring of yours gone. I've worried time and again about it getting infected, you know. Besides that, it doesn't look all that sanitary on someone working with food."

"Granny!" she exclaimed in laughing protest, though she wasn't really surprised. The elderly lady had come to an age where she said exactly what she thought, and devil take the hindmost.

"I didn't mean to hurt your feelings, but—the truth is the truth, dear."

No doubt it was, Zeni thought, and wondered if she'd ever be able to wear the ring again without remembering it.

"Zenobia! Where's our Zenobia?"

That call, impatient and harried, reverberated under the building's metal roof. It was a moment before Zeni realized they were actually paging her. The implied demand for instant obedience put her on the defensive. She wasn't used to being addressed that way, had never been used to it even before she came to Chamelot. And in recent months, she'd been the boss, or the next thing to it, at the Watering Hole.

"They've got your name all wrong, but I think it's you that Derek and his people want, sweetie. Here, let me hold your shoulder bag while you're busy."

"If you don't mind," Zeni answered. She rose to her feet with an unhurried flexing of thigh muscles then called out in clear tones. "I'm here."

The group that was busy under the brilliant lights and amid a tangle of cables, booms and cameras, parted as if at a royal command. Derek Peabody turned to locate her, searching the gathering of extras with an irritated scowl.

Seeing her, he started forward with both hands outstretched.

"Zeni, my Zenobia," he said, dropping his voice to a deep, caressing note. "How stunning you look, perfectly gorgeous. But then, I knew you would. My eye for a face never fails. The camera will absolutely make love to you, having itself a digital orgasm."

She might not be familiar with L.A. or the movie business, but Zeni knew bull when she heard it. She lifted her chin, and her voice turned cool. "Thank you. I think. Now what am I supposed to do?"

"What majesty, excellent! You're already in character. Come now. Stand just over here, on this mark, and let me tell you what the test is all about."

As she was led away, Zeni glanced back at Granny Chauvin. The elderly lady was clapping her hands while her eyes danced. But she stopped almost immediately and began to search in her purse, digging out her cell phone. High-tech-granny, that was her. No telling who she was calling.

"What we have here is a scene from the lead actor's dream. He's a football quarterback pulling down megabucks as a star in the NFL, one who makes a habit of dating sweet young things. But he's secretly into one dominant, bad-ass woman, and that's the kind he sees in his dreams. In this one, he meets a grand female who has kicked the Romans out of her country and then conquered a nice slice of the known world. That's you, love, the great Warrior Queen, Zenobia, who ruled from sand-choked Palmyra about 200

AD, more or less." He flipped his hand back and forth to indicate the unimportance of this historical fact.

"You will be playing the quarterback," Zeni said, her gaze steady.

"I will, but not today, my darling Zeni. You can pretend I'm there—you know how to do that, right?"

"If necessary. But I didn't receive the lines from your assistant as promised."

"They won't be needed!" That comment, laden with acid condescension, came from the shadows. It was followed into the light by the tall, Amazonian blonde Zeni had seen at the casting call and later at the Watering Hole.

Derek turned from Zeni to put a hand on the blonde's arm. "This is Bettina, darling Zeni, my personal assistant who makes certain I have whatever I need. You will be seeing a lot of each other during filming."

The woman offered her hand, a negligent gesture that she turned into a challenge by the strength of her grip. That mannish attempt to intimidate, added to the five extra inches the woman had on her, was more than irritating. Zeni smiled and held her own in the contest. She might not have logged as many gym hours as Bettina seemed to have put in, but she worked hard and had the muscles to show for it.

It was satisfying when the woman narrowed her eyes in something like surprise before releasing her and stepping back.

"Bettina is quite right about the lines, sweetheart," Derek went on as if nothing had happened. Laying a hand on Zeni's shoulder, he kneaded it in a caressing, almost possessive gesture. "I want you to improvise. Become Zenobia! Don the crown and regalia in imagination, and then turn and blast the hunk who has intruded into the bedroom of your palace."

"Bedroom?"

"What did you expect? The throne room? Sure, he's in your bedroom. It's his dream, you know, so where the hell else is a jock with an overload of testosterone going to go?"

"No one stops him? I mean, what about guards?"

"It's a dream, darling. All obstacles magically disappear. But the point is you're not happy to see him. In fact, you're incensed at the intrusion. Channel Queen Victoria with a side of Lady Gaga. Whatever." He clapped his hand together with a sharp crack. "Now let's see it!"

Easy for him to say; not at all easy to do.

If Zeni had known the test was going to be conducted this way, she'd have been better prepared. There had been no hint. Even more unnerving was the advance of the cameras as the actor/director stepped way, silent behemoths with their single eye trained on her. Not a single word surfaced in her mind, much less anything resembling dialogue. She simply stood there while the technicians waited beyond the glow of the bright lights that were trained on her.

The assistant, Bettina, made a sound of disgust. Peabody, standing in the shadowy region behind the main camera, began to frown down at his shoes. He folded his arms over his chest and rocked back on his heels. Off to the side, Granny Chauvin lifted a hand to her mouth while her eyes widened.

It was then that Zeni heard Trey's bike rumbling to a stop outside. Seconds later, he appeared in the building's wide doorway, his tall, wide-shouldered body a perfectly formed male figure against the light.

She pivoted toward him as if drawn, like a sunflower to the sun. He had come, and the warm gladness of it moved over her in a flash. Regardless, her features settled into her normal defensive pride.

"What," she asked distinctly, "are you doing here?"

He ambled forward, a corner of his mouth lifting in his most engaging grin. "It's a free country."

Peabody dropped his arms and lifted his head. Zeni realized suddenly that she was doing something right. She wasn't quite sure what, but decided to go with it.

"There is no freedom in my palace except that which I ordain," she declared at her most quietly arrogant. "Go. Leave me immediately."

"Damned if I will," Trey said, an unholy silver light appearing in the gray of his eyes as he played up to her.

"I'll have you arrested!"

"You and what army? I don't see one behind you, Queenie baby."

She narrowed her eyes at that deliberate provocation. Trey knew very well that she hated being called baby or any variation on the term.

"I have only to call, and they will appear."

"Fine. Do it. But it's my dream. Are you sure they'll come?"

"As sure as I am that you're a dead man," she declared, drawing herself up in the way Trey had approved there at his old house.

The sharp crack of hands starting to clap stopped them.

"Excellent," Peabody called out hard on the sound, moving toward them into the light. "That was excellent. I believe we have our Zenobia."

Relief flooded through Zeni so fast and strong that her smile in his direction was warm and unguarded. "It was really okay?"

"Indeed it was. I hope you are as pleased as I am, darling Zeni."

Her smile faded as he moved in close beside her. Was she pleased? It was hard to say. Success was better than failing, but she wasn't exactly thrilled at the prospect of enduring all this critical attention again when it was for real.

She turned her gaze to Trey almost without thinking. He gave her a thumbs-up, but made no effort to join her in the limelight. A second later his attention was deflected as Granny Chauvin walked up beside him, circling his waist in a quick hug as she said something about being glad that he answered her call.

"Who is your friend?" Peabody asked, some of the warmth draining from his voice.

"My boss, Trey Benedict. You met him at the coffee shop, I believe."

"So I did. I've also met the Benedict who is the sheriff and the one who owns Windwood Plantation where we'll be shooting a couple of scenes."

She gave a quick nod. "Benedict cousins, all three of them, Mr. Peabody. And if you should need a derelict plantation house, Trey has one of those. Oh, and the older lady is Miss Myrtle Chauvin, who knows everybody who is anybody in Chamelot, and is related to most of them."

"Derek, please, since we'll be working together."

Her smile was brief. "Derek, then."

"And now I believe I should get closer acquainted with your supporters here."

The actor put his hand to the small of Zeni's back as he moved forward at a languid pace. It made Zeni a little uncomfortable for some reason, but she walked the few steps at his side. Her thoughts were on how Trey might take this cozy approach.

She was given no time to explain. Derek gave Granny a slight bow. "Miss Chauvin, a very great pleasure." Turning, he put out his hand in direct contrast to how he'd acted the first time he and Trey met. "Nice to see you again, Benedict. I believe your arrival just now was timely for Zeni's test."

"I doubt she needed me." Trey's gaze was level and more than a little assessing as he completed the handshake.

Granny Chauvin flicked his arm with the backs of her fingers. "Of course she did. Our Zeni having so much practice at putting you in your place, it was only natural for her to give you what for!"

"Natural indeed." Derek's smile was thin. "That being the case, Benedict, I wonder if I might interest you in the part of a palace guard in this scene. It won't be a speaking role, understand. You merely enter at Queen Zenobia's call, looking grim and protective, and then stand behind her for the duration."

"Oh, I don't think—" Zeni began as she saw the hardening of Trey's jaw muscles, a sure sign of his annoyance.

"I love it," Granny declared. "Trey's good at that look."

Derek slanted Zeni a glance shaded with intimacy. "If you don't want him at your back, that's the end of it, of course."

"It isn't that."

"She would never even think such a thing, much less say it." Granny snorted, looking at Derek with disfavor.

"The part suits me fine," Trey said in abrupt, deep-voiced acceptance.

Zeni swung her head sharply to stare at him. "It does?"

"What? You thought you were the only actor in this town?" He actually grinned at her.

"No, but—"

"Hey, there's me, too," Granny chimed in.

"Besides," Trey went on, "I did agree to help you with this thing any way I can."

Zeni met his gray gaze, her own inquiring as she tried to decide why he'd accepted Derek's offer. It wasn't like him, not by a long shot. She'd have sworn he'd run a mile from a movie set, that he'd have no use for the smallest sliver of Hollywood glory.

He was up to something; she could feel it in her bones.

She just didn't know what.

CHAPTER SIX

*T*rey didn't like anything about this movie deal. The way Peabody had latched onto Zeni set his teeth on edge, and he was especially unhappy with how the man kept putting his hand on her as they talked and the hint of lewd anticipation in his expensive capped-teeth smile. Movie people might call each other dear and darling, but it didn't sound at all right applied to Zeni, not when she wouldn't even let him call her baby.

So he was a dog in the manger, so what? He didn't intend to stand back and do nothing while some smooth-talking son of a gun used Zeni for recreational sex while he was in Chamelot. He'd heard about these guys with their casting couches, their sense of entitlement and power that made any female who came into their orbit fair game.

Not Zeni, not if he could help it. He was blocking that, one way or another. Yeah, and whether she liked it or not.

Trey held her gaze for a long second, seeing the doubt about his decision there, also the suspicion. It didn't matter. She might figure out what he was doing—and probably would, as she was smarter than average—but there wasn't much she could do about it. At least, he hoped there wasn't.

"You about done here?" he asked. "I can give you a lift back to the coffee shop."

It was Peabody who answered for her. "It will be a while before she's ready. There's paperwork to be filled out."

"For all of us, I expect."

That comment came from Granny, trying to help him out, bless her sweet old heart.

"Afterward, then," he said with finality, and sent a look Peabody's way that he'd have to be a fool not to interpret.

Of course, there was no saying the guy wouldn't turn out to be the king of fools.

"Yes, well, you and our new palace guard will need to see the receptionist in the main building, Miss Chauvin. I'll take care of Zeni."

He'd just bet he would, Trey thought. Something hot and hard settled in his chest as he saw Peabody wrap his fingers around her upper arm. "No hurry to make this gig official for me," he drawled. "I'll just tag along wherever she's going."

"I thought I made it clear your paperwork will be elsewhere."

"I'm in no hurry. Waiting on that until everything's settled for Zeni isn't a problem." The actor's grip on Zeni's arm must have tightened. Trey watched with secret amusement as she freed it with a sudden twist, giving Peabody one of her looks so freezing that it should have come with an overcoat.

"I'm not sure I understand the concern. It's just a matter of a few forms to be filled out."

The irritation and condescension in Peabody's voice set Trey's stubbornness in concrete. "Then you shouldn't mind me tagging along."

"Or me," Granny said, a frown adding to the network of fine lines in her face. "I'm in no hurry, either."

"Really, this is ridiculous." The actor glanced around then lowered his voice as he noticed half the movie crew had their heads turned in their direction, listening even as they went about their business. "One would think you didn't trust her to be alone with me."

"It's not her that I don't trust," Trey said evenly.

"That's an unwarranted insult. And I fail to see why you would make it when none of this is your business."

Trey wanted to punch him. He did the next best thing. "And I fail to see why you're so set on taking my bride-to-be somewhere without me."

The actor reared back. "Bride?"

"*Bride.*" Granny breathed that pertinent word as if awestruck.

"That's right."

Trey refused to look at Zeni for fear of what he might see. Still he reached to take her hand, drawing her to his side. She came without resistance, though he wasn't sure it was because she appreciated the rescue or that she was shocked out of her wits.

"I didn't realize." The words had a petulant sound, as if Peabody felt he'd been wronged in some way.

"Obviously not." Trey tucked Zeni's hand over his arm and covered it with his own. "If you want to rethink the casting for the dream sequence—"

"No, that won't be necessary." Peabody gave a dismissive wave of one hand so his manicured and polished nails flashed in the dim light. "Zeni will be the perfect Zenobia, and I can see you will be a definite asset as her protector."

Trey wondered briefly if he'd misjudged the man. He'd taken him for the kind who would retaliate for the inter-ference with his plans and, especially, the slight to his ego. The most obvious revenge would have been to rob Zeni of her role in hope she'd take her disappointment out on her supposed husband-to-be. Did the fact that Peabody was keeping them both on mean he was a good guy?

No. No way in hell; the hard look in Peabody's eyes told him that much. What did it mean, then, that he was holding his fire?

It meant he hadn't given up, of course. He not only had designs on Zeni, still, but enticing her away from a fiancé would be even greater sport for him.

The man would be content with seeing that she paid later for any damage to his ego.

Yet Peabody was overlooking an important aspect of this arrangement, as Trey saw with no difficulty whatever. It could be a major impediment to whatever plan he might hatch, one he'd meet head-on if he wasn't careful.

That problem was Zeni, herself. She was clear-eyed, hard to fool, and had no patience with idiots.

Trey could almost feel for the guy. He saved his compassion for himself, however, since he knew he'd have to face her over this business sooner or later.

As it happened, he didn't have long to wait. She jumped him as soon as their paperwork was finished and they'd waved Granny Chauvin out of the fairgrounds parking lot.

"What was that bride-to-be business about back there?" she demanded as they stood on either side of his bike. "Have you lost it?"

"Now, don't get all excited—"

"I'm not excited yet, believe me. I just want to know what you thought you were doing."

She looked so different, softer and more accessible, as she stood there in her white, gray and black outfit, her hair drifting around her shoulders while the slanting autumn sun picked out rich auburn highlights among the warm brown strands. It was an illusion, and he'd best not forget it.

Reaching for his helmet, he tucked it under his arm before handing her the extra he always carried. It made a fine excuse for not meeting her hot gaze. "Protecting you."

"Protecting me."

"That joker seemed determined to take you away somewhere for who knows what—I thought you might not go for it."

Zeni was staring at him as if she'd never seen him before. Trey knew he'd put his foot in it, but saw no reason to back-track now. "I know you're a big girl, and all that, but

I wouldn't trust Peabody as far as I could throw him. He's the kind who takes it for granted every woman is willing to give it up to him."

"And you know this how?"

"I recognize the type. And I'm a guy."

He straddled his Harley, which put them practically nose to nose. Big mistake. His brain went a little haywire at being that close. She still wore her exaggerated screen makeup that made her look amazing. He'd checked out her mouth about a hundred times since he'd walked into the building where she'd been doing that double-damned screen test. It made his mouth water with the need to see if it tasted as delicious as it looked.

"You're a guy," she repeated, her eyes black-coffee hot. "Does that mean you make a habit of enticing women out to your old mansion? Oh, wait, maybe it does. I was there, after all."

"Nothing happened, which should prove something." He could feel the burn at the back of his neck at the thought of what could have taken place out there in that sad old house with no one around for miles.

"It doesn't, not at all, since we've never been anything more than employer and employee. Until now."

"And friends," he said at his most mulish.

She blinked a little at that, but didn't back down. "You do realize, don't you, that news of this backhanded proposal of yours will be all over town before lunch time?"

"It wasn't a proposal, backhanded or otherwise."

"Whatever." She waved her dismissal of that lame

comment. "I love Granny Chauvin, really I do, but you know how she likes being in the middle of things. I'll bet you anything she'll be on her phone to Lance and Beau before we get back to the coffee shop."

"No more bets," he said in firm tones as he took out his own cell. "I'll just explain how it was."

Exasperation thinned those delectable lips. "She knows how it was, since she was there. But you Benedict men are her favorite people. She loves calling you her Louisiana Knights and telling how you got the name. She won't be able to resist turning this into your downfall."

"Downfall? What downfall? I've never claimed to be against marriage."

"Some kind of secret engagement that she saw exposed, then. You know what I mean."

He did, and she was right, as much as he hated to admit it. Granny was a little hung up on the Knights idea. An old-fashioned romantic at heart, she was sentimental about the story of three girls who, some thirty odd years before, had all been friends, all experienced participants in the annual medieval fair, all pregnant at the same time. They'd made a pact to name their babies for ancient knights if they turned out to be boys, and so they had. Sheriff Lance Benedict was legally Lancelot, Beau carried a double whammy of names, Galahad Beauregard, and he, himself, had become Tristan, which his older sister's childhood lisp had turned into Trey. Granny liked to say the fighting they had to do to survive the monikers had made them the men they'd become. Some days, he thought she was right.

"Granny will understand," he insisted. "I'll make sure of it."

"Lovely. That will help so much in dealing with Derek," she returned without missing a beat.

"Derek?" The word sounded pained, but he couldn't help it.

"Yes, Derek. He suggested a first name basis since we'll be working closely together."

"I'm sure he did."

"And so will you. Be working with him, I mean," she went on in exasperation. "I don't know which surprised me more, that he offered the part or that you accepted it."

He looked down his nose at her. "I had to keep an eye on you, didn't I?"

"Oh, please." She didn't quite give him an eye-roll, but it was a close thing.

"Besides, half the town has been tapped for the movie. Why should I miss out on the fun?"

"It's not your thing." She began to count the reasons on her fingers. "You don't like being put on the spot. You have businesses to run. You'd far rather be riding in a dirt bike race in your spare time than standing around in makeup and a toga. Do I need to go on?"

Only one word registered. "Toga? You mean one of those short dresses?"

"It's not a dress. I don't know exactly what you'll wear, but it will have to be a costume of some kind."

He hated the sound of that, but it was too late to turn back now. "Whatever, as long as I get to stand around as a guard wherever you are."

"I don't need a guard, just as I don't need a fiancé," she insisted, her voice rising.

"Wait a minute," he said with a mock frown. "You don't think I'll have to wax the hair on my legs, do you?"

The look she gave him hovered between annoyance and outrage. "This isn't funny! We can't simply ignore what you've done."

"I don't intend to ignore it," he said at once. "As far as I'm concerned, we're engaged until this movie business is over and done, and *darling* Derek is gone. Then you can announce to the world that you don't want to be my wife, and that will be the end of it."

"Really? And I'm to go on working at the Watering Hole afterward as if nothing happened? Nobody will think that's at all strange?"

He made a sound between a laugh and a grunt. "When did you start caring what people think? Anyway, it's our business, not theirs."

Her gaze was direct, yet shadowed with something that might have been pain. "People have a way of making things their business. They'll be asking if we've set a date, can they come to the wedding, maybe where it will be held and where we'll live afterward."

"So we'll just say we haven't decided." He clapped his helmet on his head and snapped the chin strap.

"You have it all figured out, don't you?"

"No," he said with a deliberate grin, "but I think the two of us can handle it."

She stared at him for long seconds, her face softening. But then her eyes narrowed. "You're assuming that I'll go along with this crazy scheme. Also, that I have no interest in going anywhere with Derek or seeing the inside of his motor home."

"Will you? Do you? Or am I wasting my time?"

"Wouldn't you like to know?" she answered, lowering her lashes as she donned her own helmet and moved around to climb on behind him.

There it was, Trey saw with resignation, the payback for putting her in this uncertain position with his impulsive announcement. If she wasn't to know exactly what he'd been thinking when he made it, she didn't intend for him to know how she felt about it.

He might be wrong; that might not be her purpose at all. But if it was, it was working for her.

Speechless. Zeni had been absolutely speechless when Trey told Derek she was engaged to him. For the briefest of moments, she'd been lost in incredible euphoria that Trey cared enough to make that claim.

It hadn't lasted.

In the next second, she'd been sure it was a joke, that any minute he'd laugh and say no, not really; that he'd been making a point or some such thing.

That hadn't happened. It became clear, instead, that he'd gone into over-protective mode and intended to hold to his declaration. He hadn't recanted, and now he was stuck with the situation. The two of them were stuck with it.

Where had he come up with such an idea? It was one thing to suspect Derek of having designs on her, but something else for Trey to maintain he had the right to go wherever she went. He could have just said he felt responsible since she worked for him, or that he was acting in lieu of family, like a brother who meant to see no one took advantage of her. That was nearer the mark, anyway.

Wasn't it?

What he'd done seemed to shed new light on their trip out to his granddad's old place. She'd never even been to the modern bungalow outside town where he lived now, so that trip had been a little strange. It was a grand old place with its hint of permanency and tradition, but still. What was it called? Surely it had a name, though she'd only heard it referred to as the Old Benedict Place. Several of those existed, however, big old houses at the ends of long drives. Most needed another designation to set them apart.

She'd wondered if the renovation he intended was a signal for some new interest in hearth and home. Men didn't have a biological clock to worry about, but some leaned toward the stability of a family as they reached thirty. For them, children were the closest they would ever come to immortality, the only form of it that mattered.

But to believe such a thing suggested he'd taken her out there to see if she might want to live in the house before he spent a fortune restoring it to its former glory. She couldn't accept that at all.

Had she been a stand-in for some other woman? Were her impressions supposed to give him a hint of how this unknown female might feel? Or did he just want a few decorating ideas, suggestions for making the place livable?

That last seemed more in keeping with how he'd talked about it.

Another possibility was that she was being used as a shield. Trey could have an entanglement she knew nothing about, one he hoped to win free of by claiming to be engaged. That thought had possibilities.

Or it might have if Zeni hadn't known very well that he was not a coward. Trey hid behind no one.

Regardless of the cause, the engagement seemed to be on. Zeni could see nothing but problems coming from it. Problems and, very likely, regrets. There were things in her life she'd never mentioned to a soul. They were nobody's business but hers, or they hadn't been before. It was possible they might have to come out now.

And what then?

She'd rather not think about it.

She was tired from the morning's outing, more so than if she'd worked at the coffee shop all day. At the same time, she was hyper, barely able to stay in her skin. Playing with the kitten, Midnight, seemed to help a little, dangling a piece of ribbon and watching him bat at it, try to get it, or running her hand down his back while holding him against her chest.

She couldn't do that all day. The only other thing she knew to do was change into her usual tank top and jean skirt and get back to work.

Gloria, who had been doing double duty, working both the grill and cash register, looked up as she came through from the back after descending the rear stairs. "Girl, am I glad to see you," she exclaimed. "I'm about tired of telling people you'll be back soon to make them a hamburger, when I can do it just as well as you can!"

"Sorry to be gone so long," Zeni answered. "Though customer loyalty sounds like a good thing."

"Sure it is, when it means job security. I just wish you'd show me the secret ingredient that makes people rather eat what you cook!"

"Beats me," Zeni said at her most cheerful, and laughed as Gloria threw up her hands.

The girl was a hard worker who always had a smile for customers, and it didn't hurt that she was easy on the eyes. Zeni felt lucky to have her for backup. Every time she looked at her, however, she was reminded of a calypso song her mother had loved, one about a Brown Skin Girl. Gloria had the smoothest skin she'd ever seen, with a cinnamon undertone that went beautifully with shades of lavender, a fact she was bright enough to play to the hilt. Her lashes curled in a way no eyelash curler could duplicate and her mouth, tinted the color of wine, was so generous in its curves that her smile was a sight to behold. She was doing online classes at present, working toward a master's degree in psychology from LSU. She would be done in a couple of years. Everyone would be sorry to see her go, but go she would when she got her degree, taking off for bigger things, bigger places.

"How was the screen test?" Gloria asked. "What was Derek Peabody like? Was he as good-looking close up as he is on the screen?"

"You saw him when he came in the other evening. What did you think?"

"I was on the other side of the room, and it was only for a minute or two. Come on, give."

"Well, I really don't know." Zeni had to stop and gather her thoughts. She'd been so stressed over being on camera that she'd barely registered Derek's appearance. Not that she expected Gloria to believe it if she told her. And she certainly didn't want to get into a discussion on that subject here in the middle of the coffee shop. "He was nice enough," she said finally.

Gloria paused in her job of rolling utensils in paper napkins for dinner-time setups. "That's all you have to say about a guy voted the Sexiest Man Alive two years in a row?"

"He was very smooth, well-dressed in your basic movie star Armani, everything about him polished to a high gloss."

"But? I do hear a but coming, don't I?"

Zeni folded her lips together for a second. "He was a little too smooth. Yes, and he's not as tall or as bulked up as he looks in his movies."

"You don't mean it." The dry sound of Gloria's voice indicated she wasn't exactly surprised by this example of cinematic magic.

"And though he's an extremely attractive man, I think

I've grown too used to looking at the Benedict guys to be overly impressed."

"Aw, now."

"Sorry, but there it is."

"You're breaking my heart, really, you are." She went back to rolling utensils, but was watching Zeni so closely that she made a setup with two spoons and no fork and had to unroll it and start over.

"Cheer up." Zeni told her. "You'll see him again before this is done. He's sure to be back in here now and then. Maybe you'll wind up with a part in the movie."

"No way, uh-uh, nope. I don't have time for that stuff. I've got enough on my plate with studying and work."

"That why you didn't want to go the cattle call for extras?"

"Yeah, buddy. My life plans don't go down that road."

Zeni gave her an appraising look. "That's a shame, since you might have wound up as Zenobia. You'd make a better one, anyway, since she was from the Middle East."

"So get a spray tan," Gloria said with her rich, contralto laugh. "What I want to know is, did The Man say anything about your test before you left?"

"I got the part." Zeni gave a shrug that might have been a shade too casual.

"Yay!" Gloria did a little happy dance where she stood. "Excellent, news. I'm so proud for you."

"So did Trey."

"Say what?"

Zeni had to laugh at how fast her helper's dance came to

an end. And of course, the circumstances had to be explained along with who'd said what and why. By the time Zeni was done, she thought for sure she'd gotten out of the whole Derek inquisition.

Not so.

"This dream bit you'll be doing, it's Derek The Man you'll be working with, right? You have got to be looking forward to that."

"Not exactly." Zeni gathered up the napkin setups Gloria had done and piled them on a tray, ready to take to the tables.

"Why not? Does he have bad breath or something?"

"No, it's just that—I don't know. Something about being around him bothered me. He has an extra helping of ego that seems to take for granted everyone should know all about him. He acted as if I should be happy to go where he chose to lead me, do what he expected once we were there." Trey had said much the same thing. Hearing her feelings confirmed that way was one reason she hadn't rejected the fake engagement idea out of hand.

Gloria's eyes widened. "Derek Peabody wanted to take you somewhere? You and him? All alone?"

"It did look that way."

"I've known a few guys like that," the waitress said with a shake of her head. "Fancy men thinking you're all hot for what they've got in their pants, guys who get all like, 'Hey, girl, you a cock tease, got me all hot-to-trot for nothing,' when you don't want what they got. That, and thinking they can make you want it if they come on strong enough, long enough. Proper fools is what they are."

"You've got it. I hope you stay far away from that kind."

"Yes, ma'am, you better believe it."

Zeni had tried to convince Gloria to drop the ma'am business. She was only a couple of years older, after all. More than that, she and Trey were on such relaxed terms that expecting formality from Gloria would be ridiculous. The girl had finally come around where she was concerned, except when her feelings were touched or she meant to emphasize a point. She used the honorific for Trey most of the time, however, since he was the boss. She had strong ideas about how things should be, and wasn't about to change them.

Thinking about that, Zeni was reminded of how irritated Trey had been at her use of Derek's first name. She'd thought nothing of it at first; the suggestion from the actor/director seemed no more than a friendly gesture. She could see now that it established a quick intimacy between them, along with the implication that closeness might increase.

Or did it? It was possible she was overthinking the incident, letting her outlook be swayed simply because Trey didn't trust Derek. She would have to take careful note next time they were together, to see what she really thought.

That wouldn't be for several days. Filming for the movie might begin next week, but the dream sequence wasn't exactly a major scene; it was sure to come later in the schedule.

That was all right. Zeni was in no hurry.

CHAPTER SEVEN

"What is this about you and Trey being engaged? And why is it we have to hear the news second hand?"

The questions, half joking and half serious, came from Carla Benedict as she marched into the coffee shop. She was two steps ahead of her husband Beau who held the door for her then let it ease shut behind him.

Gloria turned on Zeni with a fist propped on one hip and wrath in her dark chocolate eyes. "Say what? You've been standing right here beside me for half an hour and said not one word?"

Caught out already, Zeni saw with resignation. How to answer? She could hardly deny it, not without contradicting Trey and making nothing of what he'd tried to do for her. But accepting it would make it official.

While she made up her mind, she took chocolate muffins that Carla and Beau always ordered from the keeper and poured cups of coffee to go with them. Speaking over her shoulder, she said finally, "It's no big deal."

"I beg to differ," Carla corrected. Bright and vivacious, with honey brown hair and sea-colored eyes, she was a former magazine editor who now wrote travel guides, so could get away with saying things like that.

"So do I." Beau wiped crumbs from someone's lunch sandwich from the seat of a counter stool for his wife, and then slid onto the one next to it. "Trey popping the question is a huge deal."

That the pair had opted for the counter instead of taking a table was a sure sign they didn't intend to drop the subject. Zeni faced them with a wry smile. "It only happened a couple of hours ago. I'm still in shock."

"You mean to say he proposed this morning?" Gloria demanded.

Zeni laughed a little, trying to make light of it all. "Oh, he didn't exactly propose."

"And how was that?" Carla asked as she began to peel the paper from her muffin.

"You'll have to ask Trey." That was the best Zeni could think of at the moment.

"Ask me what?"

The question came from the man himself as he walked out of the back storeroom, looking as if all was right with his world. He didn't pause, but moved behind the counter and took the coffee pot from the warmer to pour himself a cup.

It was Gloria who answered him, her expression accusing. "Folks here want to know why you didn't propose to

Zeni the way you should, making a production out of it. You think you didn't have to because she should jump at the chance to be Mrs. Tristan Thomas Benedict?"

"Gloria!" Zeni said in protest. "It wasn't as if I was complaining."

Trey met her eyes, his own gray gaze measuring. "Maybe you should have been. To be asked is your right, after all."

"Not really," she said, uncomfortable at being the center of attention, not to mention uncertain of where he was going with it. "I mean, it isn't as if—"

"Oh, but it is. And I need to do something about that."

Setting his coffee cup aside, he reached for Zeni, drawing her into the circle of his arms and clasping his hands at her lower back. "Zeni Medford, will you do me the honor of becoming my wife?"

She could hardly refuse after everything they'd said earlier, wouldn't have even if it hadn't been such a public proposal. Still, this wasn't how she'd thought she might hear those words one day. She'd pictured privacy and deep emotion, maybe moonlight and whispers of love along with promises of forever. Not that this was the real thing, but it seemed lacking, regardless.

"Good grief, Trey," Carla said with humor in her voice. "Aren't you forgetting something?"

"What?" Trey asked, though Zeni had to give him credit for never taking his attention from her face. She knew that, because she was watching him, absorbing the warmth in the depths of his eyes, as well as the firmness of his body against her and the strength of his arms that held her.

"That you love her desperately and can't live without her, for a start," Carla suggested.

"Carla, honey," Beau began.

"Well, it's nothing compared to all the things you said to me," she answered, her voice bright with laughter as she answered her husband.

"Besides, it's about time," Gloria put in then. "I've been thinking you two should get together ever since I started work here."

Carla gave a firm nod. "Same here, only longer."

"Right you all are," Trey answered without hesitation, while his hold on her tightened. "I love you deeply, devotedly, and, yes, desperately, dearest Zeni, and can't bear the thought of life without you. Say you'll marry me before this crew makes me get down on one knee."

She tilted her head to one side as she pretended to think for a long second, but then heaved a sigh. "Since you put it so nicely, I guess so."

"I take that as a yes," he said on a laugh that she felt as much as heard. Then swinging her to halfway around so she was draped backward over his arm, he set his mouth to hers.

Her world spun in wild circles, wobbling on its axis, while her heart beat up into her throat. The kiss, unlike the proposal, felt real. She was immersed in the feel, scent and taste of him, dizzy with the sudden overload of her senses. She clung to him to keep from falling, but also because he was the only thing solid and trustworthy within her reach.

As he lifted his head after long, breathless moments, and

then shifted her upright again, she stared up at him, flushed and unbelieving. "You—you—" she began as she sought for words to blast him without embarrassing them both more than he had already.

"No, you don't," he said in husky satisfaction. "You said yes, and you can't take it back. I have witnesses."

"What you have is a colossal nerve," she began.

"I do, and you can tell me all about it later, but right now, we should be celebrating." He looked up. "Shouldn't we, Gloria."

"Yes, sir, champagne coming right up." The waitress headed toward the back storeroom with a grin on her face, making for the refrigerated wine cabinet that had been installed a short while back.

It was Asti Spumante instead of champagne, since they kept several bottles for an elderly Italian gentleman who came in every Saturday night and had it after his meal. It didn't matter. Trey toasted Zeni and their future together, she saluted their friends, the town and the Watering Hole where she'd met Trey, and the laughter, congratulations and exchanges of views and quips were free and easy.

It was so spontaneous and heartwarming that Zeni felt the rise of tears along with the furtive wish that the occasion could be something more than pretense. To become a true part of Trey's life, joining the ranks of the wives and sincere ladyloves of the Benedict Knights, would be beyond dreams. She could ask for nothing more magical.

Too bad. This wasn't real, no matter how she might yearn for it to be that way.

So she smiled and joked and, every now and then, sent a verbal jab Trey's way just to keep thing from getting too serious. He took them with a rueful smile, but something in his eyes promised retribution that made her shiver in anticipation.

In a preemptive strike, she said to Carla and Beau, "Granny Chauvin told you Trey finagled a part in this movie, I expect. But did she tell you he'll be wearing a dress for it?"

"A toga," Trey put in at once, a pained look on his face. "You promised that wasn't the same thing."

Ignoring that, she went on, "Or maybe it will be Bedouin robes like Lawrence of Arabia. Who knows?"

Carla turned to stare at him. "What do you want to bet he turns up looking like the Sheikh of Araby."

Zeni laughed at her droll, half-lascivious tone of voice. "With a turban and big old diamond right in the middle of his forehead?"

"And a scimitar at his side," Beau suggested, getting into the spirit of the thing by singing that bit from an old, fairly non-PC, country and western song about Ahab, the Arab.

Trey lifted a brow in his cousin's direction. "Traitor. But that's actually good. I've always wanted to wield a scimitar."

Zeni turned to Carla again as a thought struck her. "I didn't see you and Mandy this morning. Weren't you two chosen for parts at the cattle call?"

"Extras only," she answered with a shake of her head. "No special roles like you and Granny Chauvin. We were rushed through our registration and instructions the same day."

"Yes, well, that's all I wanted when this thing started."

Even as she made that point, she caught the question that Beau, across from her, put to Trey.

"Speaking of scimitars, swords and so on, how's the medieval fair coming along? You think too many of the town's resources are being diverted to the movie company?"

"Things aren't coming together quite as well as in other years," Trey answered. "Last I heard, the committee was thinking of canceling the ring tournament."

Beau gave a nod. "I heard that, too. Something about not being able to gather up enough horses trained to gallop down the arena with lances waving around their heads?"

"Hard to believe. The country just south of here is full of cattle herds and Cajun cowboys. Of course, they could be staying away from all the movie folderol."

"No problem," Beau said, grinning even as he glanced toward the front door when its bell jangled a warning of new arrivals. "They could always substitute motorcycles for the horses."

"Yeah, right. That would be totally medieval."

"But just picture it, cuz, you and your biker buds in shiny armor, thundering down the arena. There are picking up speed, kicking up sand, guiding your bike with your left while leveling a lance under your right arm. You spear the ring and the crowd goes wild—I can see it now!"

Zeni barely heard Trey's rather profane comment as she looked toward the door. Her nerves, which had almost relaxed, tightened into knots again.

"I can see that, as well," Derek said as he strolled toward the counter. "I like it. I like it a lot. What will it take to make it happen?"

Trey's first impulse was to throw the actor out and ban him from the premises. He could do it; he was irritated enough and the Watering Hole belonged to him, after all.

Peabody might be speaking to him and Beau, but it was obvious he'd come to see Zeni. A distinctly sour look had crossed the actor/director's face as he saw her standing shoulder to shoulder with him, her supposed husband-to-be. Peabody's cool blue stare flicked back and forth between the two of them like the tongue of a snake testing the atmosphere.

"Well, now," Trey said, "I expect you'll have to take that up with the mayor and her fair committee."

"I'll do that, though I foresee no particular difficulty. I assume I'll have your cooperation if the proper permission is granted?"

"Mine?" Trey could play dumb with the best of them when it suited his purpose.

Peabody's smile was thin. "I believe you're the president of the local motorcycle gang—or club, I should say. I'd think you would be the go-to person for arranging a run-through of this competition and its eventual filming?"

The actor, or more likely his minions, had been checking up on him. What did that mean, exactly? "You make up your mind fast, don't you?"

"It's a habit that's stood me in good stead in a cut-throat business."

No doubt it had, but he didn't have to preen himself about it. "That's fine, but I don't know about this deal. The club is made up of a bunch of guys who like Harleys and enjoy riding on weekends, with maybe a cross-country trip now and then. We're not stuntmen."

"But you would be paid stuntmen rates, as well as being seen in the final film. Your group might like these perks. What do you say?"

"I say you'd be better off with professionals. Your insurance company might not be too thrilled if some of us amateurs got hurt." Putting obstacles in the man's way was second nature; Trey didn't even have to think about it.

"That's my worry, isn't it?" Peabody returned. "All you have to do is get out there and show your—ah, horsepower."

The man was the backend of a horse himself, in Trey's opinion. "We'll see."

"So we shall." The actor's smile was the epitome of confidence. "Next time you're at the fairgrounds, I'll see you're measured for the armor."

Armor on a bike, heavy, rigid, movement constricting armor? Trey shuddered to think of it, given that balance and agility often made the difference between control and loss of it.

Peabody turned from him to Zeni, giving her his order for coffee and a slice of her coconut pie with the mile-high meringue. Weird, but Trey wanted to deck him for that, too.

He'd watched her take orders from men a thousand times, but this was different.

He didn't want her serving the actor/director in any capacity whatsoever. That was the long and short of it.

"Gloria?" he said, and gave the waitress a straight look while tipping his head toward the movie man.

"Yes, sir," she said at once.

The girl was quick and smart as a whip. Taking the coffee pot from Zeni that she'd just picked up, she bumped her aside with one hip and took over the order.

Peabody left a short time later, when it became obvious he had no chance of carving out time alone with his Zenobia. At least, Trey assumed that was it, as he looked frustrated as hell. Beau and Carla followed soon after, with a backward glance or two that said they thought he and Zeni might like a little privacy. Quitting time for Gloria arrived, and she left to go study before joining an online conference for one of her classes.

It was the slack period for the coffee shop, after lunch and before happy hour. He and Zeni actually had the place to themselves, at least temporarily. Trey waited with some anticipation for the explosion sure to come.

Zeni glance at him, and then away again. "We missed lunch," she said. "Do you want a hamburger or something?"

Was that all she had to say? He was disappointed for some strange reason.

"Not right now. But you go ahead."

"I'm not hungry either."

"All this is enough to kill your appetite, all right."

She gave him a dark look, then picked up a damp dish cloth and began wiping the counter top. He watched her get rid of crumbs and water rings, and then drop the cloth into the sink to wash the glass coffee pot she'd emptied and dunked into the sudsy water.

The way she handled the slippery glassware, with gentle yet firm control, the way the warm white lather slid over her hands, was almost unbearably sensuous. Trey felt a tightening in his lower abdomen and closed his eyes in exasperation. Everything she did turned him on these days.

It was all he could do to keep his face bland and unconcerned when she let the dish water out of the sink, wrung out her cloth and hung it to dry, and then turned to look at him.

"What was the big idea just now, proposing like that?" she asked, crossing her arms over her chest and leaning one hip against the counter. "Wasn't it enough to tell them we were engaged? Did you have to give them a lip-lock demonstration?"

"Lip-lock," he repeated, bemused by the term. It was so descriptive, yet lacking when it came to the kiss they'd shared.

"You know what I mean, so don't try to distract me. I hate being in this position."

"As my bride-to-be." He wanted to be absolutely clear before he started explaining.

"Pretend bride," she said with every sign of loathing. "Fooling Gloria, your friends, and everybody else in town about what's between us. Or what's not."

"Fooling Peabody."

"I'm not sure he's fooled at all, or else he doesn't give a damn."

Trey gave her a tight look. "If he bothers you too much, let me know."

"And you'll do what? Bloody his nose?"

"Maybe, since he's extra protective of that surgical wonder."

She scowled at him. "If a woman had said that, she'd be labeled catty."

"Just call me Midnight's pal."

She refused to be deflected by humor. "Lay a finger on Derek, and he'll have you arrested for assault before you can turn around."

"Or not, since I have close connections with the sheriff's office," Trey returned at once.

"Which won't matter if he calls in a big city law firm."

He lifted a shoulder. "It could be worth a few months in jail."

"Don't say that!"

"Why Zeni, it's almost as if you cared." He watched her with a certain amount of sympathy since he knew he was being obtuse.

"I'd rather not have to visit you there."

"You'd come see me?"

"I'd have to or leave town," she said with scathing precision. "People here would never understand if I abandoned you, not after you going to jail for defending my honor."

The drama of that almost made him smile. "Don't worry.

It's not going to happen. Peabody has a movie to make and a career to protect. He'll film what he wants and then he'll leave. And that will be that."

"Maybe." She gave him a dark look. "But then we'll have to fix this mess you've made."

"Hey, you almost sound as if you'd rather see me in prison."

"It's a thought," she said before drowning out any reply he might have made by punching the start button on the industrial-sized dishwasher he'd installed to save her the time and effort of washing up three times a day.

She didn't mean it; Trey knew that very well. She was just worried, chafing against the situation he'd created. He liked that about her, that she felt the pretense was wrong. It didn't much bother him, however, not if it kept Peabody at bay.

He wasn't worried in any case. She'd be all right no matter how things turned out; he would see to that personally.

Meanwhile, he'd had his kiss, the one he'd fantasized about for months. He'd had it, been swept away by it to the point of forgetting their audience, and she hadn't slugged him afterward. He considered that a win.

He should be satisfied. Not likely.

All he could think of was holding her again. Yes, and maybe brushing his lips across the tattoo on her back and then over her shoulder to her breasts, kissing every inch of her before sinking so deep inside her that he could feel her heartbeat.

He wanted her. He'd wanted her for ages, wanted her to

stop frowning at him and be happy to see him, to stop snipping at him and say—what? That she loved him deeply, devotedly and desperately?

He was the one who'd said that. And if need be, he might say it again.

CHAPTER EIGHT

The mayor and the medieval fair committee were pushovers. Either that or geniuses. They agreed to allow the modern element of motorcycles in the ring tournament but, in return, insisted on the parade that led off the festivities being filmed for use as background while the movie's credits rolled. If the footage made it into theaters, it should be invaluable promotion for Chamelot's future fairs.

Trey went around tight-lipped and out of sorts after hearing about the agreement, but soon fell into line with doing his civic duty. Over the next week, he and eight of his biker buddies, including Jake Benedict, another cousin from over toward Turn-Coupe, spent hours in a field outside town. There they practiced guiding their bikes with one hand and holding onto lances borrowed from the medieval fair committee with the other.

Riding back and forth at top speed, they vied with each other, attempting to skewer one of the metal rings dangling from lines attached to a makeshift support—though it looked more like a goalpost than the traditional archway for the tournament. It was hot and dusty work in the extended Indian summer they were having, and the whole crew was in and out of the Watering Hole often. Over water, coffee and cold draft, they held loud and longwinded discussions about the best lance lengths to carry, the maximum speed for effect and efficiency, and how to judge wind direction and velocity for the best chance of collecting rings.

The whole thing sounded dangerous to Zeni, especially after one or two of the riders limped into the place following spills. She wished she had never gone near the cattle call that had started the whole mess, never met Derek Peabody. She dreaded to see the actor walk through the door for fear he'd say something that might set Trey off, making matters worse than they were already. It was a great relief that Derek usually showed up while Trey was away.

She came close to backing out of her part at least a dozen times. What stopped her was recognizing that it would change little. The thing had gone too far.

It did help that she had the protection of the engagement; at least Derek paid lip service to it most of the time. If she sometimes suspected he saw it as a challenge, one he couldn't resist trying to overcome, she had no reason to call him on it.

How relieved she'd be when the movie and medieval fair were both done and things got back to normal. This, in spite of knowing the special moments with Trey would then be over, moments when he casually dropped an arm around her shoulders, swung her into an impromptu dance to some tune on the jukebox or wiped powdered sugar from a doughnut off her lips and then licked it from his fingers. The teasing, the touches and fleeting kisses to please the customers, gaining their good wishes and congratulations, would be through, finished. Yes, and so would the strain.

Oh, but what then?

Zeni tried not to think about that, though she sometimes caught Midnight up and held the kitten's small, soft body against her face while asking him what she was going to do. He was a good companion, always glad to see her, keeping her company while she read herself to sleep and curling against her back during the night. But he never answered her question.

As the week wound down she had a call asking her to come out to the movie location for a costume fitting. The notice made the scene she was to play more concrete. And if it made her feel sick with nerves as well, she almost thought she deserved it for getting involved in the confounded business.

It was with some trepidation that she showed up at the cheap trailer brought in to serve as the wardrobe room. The inside of the thing was basically one large, open space. An enclosed office with a single plate glass window took up one corner, with a seating area directly outside it and a door marked as a restroom just beyond. The remaining space held racks of clothing and costumes of all shapes and sizes.

The wardrobe mistress, a matronly figure wearing a smock stuck with pins over her street clothes, introduced herself as Millie. She stood back a second, looked Zeni up and down, and then turned to pull a costume from the nearest rack.

"Try this on for size, honey."

Zeni felt the stir of anger and chagrin. The outfit was far too skimpy, like some male designer's idea of what might be worn in a harem, or else the costume worn by the female genie in the old sitcom *I Dream of Jeannie.*

"I don't think that will work," Zeni said as firmly as she could manage without shouting.

"This?"

"No," she said, and repeated that single negative again, and yet again, as the wardrobe mistress presented three similar versions, one after the other.

Zeni had researched the warrior queen of the desert, so had a fair idea of what she might have worn. Nothing she'd been offered came close. She began to explain, but Millie barely listened. Replacing the rejected costumes on the rack, she took a cell from her pocket and tapped in a text message

"I think this is a problem for Derek," she said, her face set in grim lines. "He'll be here in a few minutes."

Surely he had more important matters to oversee? But that was all right. Zeni had a few things to say to him if he'd ordered the costumes she'd been shown so far.

"Is there a problem here?" the actor/director asked, mild annoyance in his voice as he came through the door.

The wardrobe mistress got in her accusation first. "According to Miss Medford, the costumes selected for her are unsatisfactory. Amazing, for a bit player."

"Zenobia was a queen, ruler of Palmyra and lands as far away as Turkey, not some female shut up in a harem," Zeni said, her gaze direct and voice level. "She considered herself on a par with the Caesars of Rome, and actually was a Roman citizen through her father's family. In most paintings, she's shown wearing clothing similar to the Romans."

"That may be, Zeni, darling," Derek said, coming forward to take her hand. "But you'll be acting in some modern guy's wet dream, not a historical epic."

"Your wet dream, you mean."

He tried to look humble, but failed. "I suppose you could say so, as I'll be playing the lead. But what does this football hero know about history or how the queen of Palmyra might have dressed? He's seeing her not as she was, but as he'd like her to be."

"There you go," Millie said, backing up her boss.

"You might as well forget Zenobia, then, and use any harem girl," Zeni replied.

"The point is that this noble warrior queen develops a yen for our modern guy, and sets out to seduce him."

"Really."

It was the first she'd heard of that development, since she'd yet to see a script. She wasn't at all sure she liked it.

"The action is meant to be an indicator of his attractiveness on one hand and the way he sees himself on the other."

Derek's looks and vision, she thought with sardonic

recognition, while brushing that argument aside. "You'll give the audience a totally false impression. Zenobia should be a role model for young girls, an example of a powerful female ruler, not some exotic bimbo."

"But the half-naked female is the fantasy of the audience—that is to say, of the frat guys who love skin mags and get off on the idea of invading a harem. We have to be reasonable."

"You may, but I don't." She turned away from Derek and the wardrobe mistress, picking up her shoulder bag from the chair where she'd left it. "This is my body we're talking about here, and I decide how much of it to show off. Yes, and also how and when."

The wardrobe mistress sucked in her breath in shock. Derek jerked his head back, less than pleased, but he recovered quickly. "You can't just quit."

"I believe I can," she said without heat.

"You don't mean you'll just—just give up this opportunity."

She didn't bother to answer, but started toward the outside door.

He was standing between her and her goal, and didn't budge. Instead, he sent a brief glance toward the wardrobe mistress. "Take a coffee break, Millie. Give us half an hour."

Zeni's nerves tightened, but she saw no need for alarm. The trailer had thin walls and was in the middle of a movie location with dozens of people shuttling back and forth around it. Regardless, she didn't put down her shoulder bag.

As the door closed behind Millie, Derek eased closer. Lifting a hand, he ran the backs of his fingers down her arm from shoulder to elbow while watching her with narrowed eyes. "You don't really want to leave, do you? This part could be the beginning of big things. We could work together on other projects, go places you've never imagined."

"I like Chamelot," she said, stepping back from him so his hand fell away. "And I'm not sure I care for the movie business if this is the way it's going to be."

"Your principles become you, my dear. But I think you'll discover that they can be a handicap when it comes to getting what you want out of life."

"That's a very cynical view."

"Rather, a useful one."

"Do you think so? I think the handicap is having so few principles you fail to understand those who cherish theirs." She made as if to move around him. "Now, if you don't mind?"

"Don't go, please. Try on a couple of the costumes. Let me see what can be done to make them more acceptable."

Did he mean that? Zeni wasn't sure. At least he backed away from her, settling onto the loveseat in the seating area. He propped an ankle over one knee, stretching out his arms along the backs of the cushions on either side of him in a pose that was probably meant to look nonthreatening.

She did see possibilities in a couple of the costumes that lined the walls, but wasn't about to make use of the flimsy screen in one corner that served as a dressing room. She considered the gender-neutral restroom, nodding to herself. A moment later, she plucked two different ensembles from where they hung. Looking them over with a critical eye, she added another. Then she whisked into the restroom with them and closed the door.

"Don't be prudish," Derek began in protest.

It was too late. Zeni snapped the lock without a care for what he might think about it. Muttering under her breath, she hung her costume choices on the hook screwed into the back of the door, then began to undress.

Ten minutes later, she was ready. Turning this way and that in front of the small mirror over the sink, she thought the amalgamation of items she'd put together hadn't turned out too badly. The heavy kohl eyeliner and other makeup she'd added, similar to that created for her screen test, was icing on the cake.

Derek gaped when she glided out of the restroom with her head held high. His mouth moved but no sound came out. She looked about right for the part, Zeni knew, but his surprise seemed excessive. All she'd done was repurpose the various costumes into something closer to what she'd seen in paintings of Zenobia online.

The result was a cream-colored, ankle-length tunic banded in gold and worn with a long purple-red stole that draped from her left shoulder, behind her back and under her right arm, and then over her left shoulder from the front. A wide, braided belt encased her hips, emphasizing her waist, while the long ends falling to the floor swung gracefully as she walked. A dagger in an embroidered scabbard hung suspended on chains from its knot. Her hair, braided and wrapped her head, supported a gold and gemstone diadem that gleamed with blue, green and red fire in the feeble overhead light.

She felt regal, she looked regal, and so she was regal.

"My God, Zeni," the actor/director said, exhaling on a quiet breath as he rose slowly to his feet.

It was fitting homage for a queen.

Trey was hot, tired, and something beyond damp when he reached the Watering Hole. He and the guys had transferred from their practice field to the rodeo arena this afternoon. Once there, they'd had to rethink their approach to this ring tournament on Harleys.

The arena at the edge of the fairgrounds had worked out well in the past, when the tournament was held on horseback, and it was probably logical from a filming standpoint. However, it wasn't designed for the feat they were expected to pull off. The run toward the big arch from which the rings would be suspended was too short. A certain amount of speed was required to hold both the bike and the lance steady on the approach to the rings, and there just wasn't enough track to reach it. Once a ring was speared, there was a high danger of hitting the arena wall due to the excess speed.

A couple of options had been proposed. They could circle the arena to pick up speed before turning onto the straightaway toward the rings, something that seemed workable. After trying for a ring, they could reduce speed and swerve in a spray of dirt to avoid the wall, or else rigged their brakes so they could be controlled by the left hand for a fast stop.

The riders had been split down the middle on the question, and the discussion had been about as cordial as the one on whether they'd all paint their bikes the same shiny black as Trey's. They'd tried the stunt both ways, more or less, and Trey had hit the wall twice, the last time hard enough to leave its mark on him and the bike. Before they could come to a final agreement, a cloud boiled up from the southwest and it started to rain.

The blessed movie was the last thing on Trey's mind just now. He was starving, since he'd missed lunch and couldn't remember what he'd had for breakfast. He was also chilled to the bone after riding from the arena in the rain while wearing jeans and a black tank top instead of his leathers. All he wanted was a cup of hot coffee, a bowl of the chili that Zeni had been making when he saw her at daybreak, then a shower and at least three solid hours in his lounge chair while he watched a ball game. A beer with the last was optional.

Zeni hit him with her proposition the minute he walked in the door.

"Hey, you think you'll have time to go over this Zenobia scene with me, maybe help me memorize my lines?"

"Do what?" He couldn't believe she expected him to agree to such a thing knowing how he felt about it. The look he gave her as he slid onto his favorite stool at the counter should have been answer enough.

"I don't mean right this minute," she said, easily matching him in exasperation. "Later, after I close down for the night. Derek handed me a copy of the script this afternoon, and I need to work on the lines and other business."

"Business?"

"Where I'm supposed to stand, how I'm to move, sit, and other bits of action."

Her use of the jargon, and how fast she'd picked it up, made him uneasy. He'd prefer she didn't get too comfortable with it. "You can't do that by yourself?"

She dished up a bowl of chili without being asked, as if she could read his mind. Maybe she could; he wouldn't be surprised. However, she didn't look at him while she was doing it.

"Not really," she said. "It's the stuff that's going on while I say my lines that I'm not sure about. I could call Derek, since he offered to go over it with me, but I'd really rather not."

"You don't want to practice with Peabody." He refused to call the guy by the name used in all the media he'd found online, the one on everybody's lips all over town. He didn't care to be that friendly.

"Rehearse," she corrected. "And no, I don't."

"How come? I mean you'll have to do the scene with him in front of the cameras sometime."

"Yes, but it doesn't have to be now. Besides, he's a busy man."

She was suddenly busy herself, bringing him crackers to go with his chili and pouring him a cup of coffee. It was easy to see something about rehearsing with Peabody bothered her. If she didn't want to be around the guy, that was probably a good thing. He didn't want the actor/director near her, either.

Why he'd pushed her about it, he didn't know. He could be an idiot like that when he was so tired he couldn't see straight.

"And I'm not a busy man?" he asked while tearing into a packet of crackers and crumbling them over his chili.

"You are, yes." She poured a glass of cold milk and shoved it down the counter, timing it so perfectly that it stopped beside his hand. "But you're also the man who lost a bet and is supposed to be helping me with this part."

"Getting it was the deal, not playing it," he answered, just to be ornery since he knew very well he was going to do what she wanted. "I thought I was done."

Putting her palms against the edge of the counter, she leaned in toward him. "I don't believe we set a time limit on the payment. Are you reneging?"

He met her hot chocolate gaze, his spoon suspended in the air and his own eyes steady. "Never."

"Good." She pushed away from the counter. "I'll see you at closing time."

Trey left soon afterward. At home, he showered, shampooed and shaved. He watched the news, found out he didn't care what was on ESPN, and took a cat nap. In spite of it all, he was in his truck and back at the Watering Hole a good half hour before he was due.

The early arrival didn't matter at all. Rain still fell, coming down heavy enough to keep most folks at home. The diehard supper group was just about finished, those who would rather get soaking wet than cook for themselves. A few stragglers were still having dessert when he walked in, but cleared out soon after.

He helped Zeni load the dishwasher, then he wiped down tables while she swept. Locking the door and turning off the open sign, he followed her up to her apartment.

Midnight came to greet them as they came through the door, weaving in and out between their legs and complaining mightily about being shut up without company. Zeni soothed the kitten a minute or two, and then fed him. Handing over a longneck beer from the refrigerator, she went to change into something that, so she said, didn't smell like coffee and grilled onions.

Trey hadn't noticed and wouldn't have cared if he had; the only fragrance he'd caught as he climbed the stairs behind her had been sweet peas and patchouli with a delectable side note of Zeni.

He made himself at home on the sofa. As he sipped his beer, he noticed the bound movie script that lay on the camphor wood coffee table. Reaching for it, he leaned back, stretched out his long legs, and opened it to the page that was marked by a sticky note.

He read through the scene, beginning slow but picking up speed with every line. He turned the page and finished the fairly short sequence, then sat without moving for long seconds. Turning back to the beginning, he read the thing through again. He chugged the rest of his beer, set the bottle aside, and read it a third time while heat radiated from the top of his head.

Trey slapped the pages shut and sat up straight. He shook his head with a low whistle. Moving with care, he dropped the script back on the table and left it there while he got to his feet.

Go or stay, that was the question. Walk out now, this very minute, while he still could—or stay and see what was going to happen?

Outside, the rain was still coming down. He could hear its splatter and splash clearly because the window above the kitchen sink was open a few inches for air circulation. The fresh scent of it permeated the apartment, bringing a hint of fragrance from the wet black-eyed Susans that grew along the building's back wall. The humid coolness of it drifted in as well, a welcome addition.

Trey moved to the kitchen window and pushed it higher so the air flow and sound of the rain increased. He stood there with his hands on the sill, breathing in the cool dampness, letting it take the heat from his thoughts and the fire from the lower part of his body.

As he stared out into the darkness, he asked himself if Zeni had any idea at all of what she was doing to him.

CHAPTER NINE

*Z*eni took a quick shower. She'd been up since daybreak, standing over a hot oven and grill and scalding dish water, but the main reason was because Trey seemed so fresh and squeaky clean he made her feel grungy by comparison. A dusting of bath powder afterward not only banished the *eau de coffee shop* smell for good, but made it easier to skim into lacy underwear and her caftan lounge robe.

The cover-up was the only thing of that variety she owned, but, most conveniently, mimicked the long tunics worn by Roman matrons, so was similar to what might have been worn by Zenobia. Nothing like getting into character for the reading, or so she'd heard somewhere, probably a TV show.

Trey had his back to her, standing at the kitchen cabinet, when she emerged from the bedroom. She was struck by the sheer male power of him, more aware than she wanted to be of how large he loomed in her apartment, the strength of his personality making it seem smaller.

It felt odd, almost illicit, to have him there so late in the evening. She wondered what the good folks of Chamelot would say if they saw his truck still parked at the Watering Hole. Maybe they wouldn't notice, since it was at the back of the building.

Then again, why should it be a problem? She and Trey were supposed to be engaged, after all. Late night visits should be expected. Wasn't it fairly well accepted these days that couples bound for the altar were intimate?

Yes, well, except whatever Trey, the bad boy Benedict, got up to was bound to be fodder for public comment, no matter what else was happening in town.

"Have you had a chance to look at the script?" he asked with a brief glance over his shoulder.

She'd thought he was oblivious, hadn't realized she was there. She'd learn not to underestimate him one day. "Why? Something wrong with it?"

"Just curious."

"No time. As I said before, it was given to me after the costume fitting today. Gloria needed to study for a test, so I took over downstairs as soon as I got back."

He tipped his head in acknowledgment. "She's doing okay with the extra hours she's working?"

"Great, I think."

Zeni gave him a quick frown as she answered. It wasn't like Trey to ask about what was happening at the coffee shop. He'd been so busy lately with the stunt for the movie along with his other responsibilities that he must be feeling a little left out of things.

It was also possible he felt out of place in the apartment. This was his second time here in the past week, which was more often than in the past year. In fact, the only other time he'd been was just after she moved in, to fix a leak under the sink. He was scrupulous about not intruding, also about shielding her from gossip.

That seemed a shame, now. It felt right to have him there, and she liked that no else was around. Wasn't that a peculiar state of affairs?

She didn't exactly mind looking at the broad expanse of his shoulders where his shirt pulled across them, either, or the lean line of his back and the tight shape of his backside as he leaned forward a bit toward the open window. Maybe she liked it too much, considering the tingling contraction of her nipples and the uncomfortable pressure between her legs.

"Look," she said, driven by a vague instinct for self-preservation, "if you'd rather not do this right now—"

He turned with deliberation, shoving his hands into his pockets as he braced his lower back against the cabinet. "No, I would rather." He grimaced. "What I mean to say is, I'm ready when you are."

Something in his voice affected her nerves like a shot of warm and sweet liqueur. It slid along her veins, lodging in her chest for a breathless instant. She met his gaze, noting a glow in their dark gray depths like the flash of lightning in a night sky, a fierceness that made her skittish, and aware once more that the two of them were supposed to be an engaged couple.

Midnight chose that moment to glide from the bedroom where he had been watching her dress from his favorite vantage point on the bed. It was a welcome distraction. As he wound around her ankles, half under the hem of her caftan, she bent to pick him up. Holding the small creature against her like a shield, she turned toward the living area.

"Fine," she said over her shoulder. "Ready to get started?"

He followed her; she could sense him behind her, as if every atom of her body was attuned to the minute particles of his. She was also super aware that she was half naked under her robe; that it would take very little to whip that covering away from her for access.

It was a disconcerting idea—not that she hadn't had such thoughts before. She had, but Trey usually wasn't around when they cropped up. If he was, she banished them with strict control.

Where that control was now, she didn't know; it seemed to have deserted her.

"Do you want to read through the scene first?" She glanced at the script on the chest that served as a coffee table.

"I did that, while I was waiting."

"What did you think?" It was just something to say; she couldn't imagine that he cared much one way or the other.

"It was—interesting."

She put Midnight on the sofa, then sat down beside the cat and reached for the bound pages. "What do you mean?"

"I have a hard time seeing why Peabody thought you were so perfect for the role."

"Really?"

"Read it," he said.

He'd stopped in the middle of the living area as if taking his place on the stage. The light from the fixture overhead caught in the waves of his hair with a blue-black sheen and gleamed along his nose, but left his eye sockets in shadow. His stance, the low sound of his voice and lack of eye contact were disturbing, though she would never admit it, not even to herself.

Midnight leapt to the cushions on the back of the sofa and then strolled noiselessly to the one directly behind her head, stretching out there as if to be close at hand in case of need. The move was oddly comforting. Turning to the script page marking her scene, Zeni began to read.

It didn't take long; it was a bit part after all. There were only six or seven lines for her and the same for the lead actor, who would be Derek, of course. She could feel the increasing throb of the pulse in her throat, sense the prickly reddening of her skin like the eruption of a rash.

"Oh my God," she whispered.

"You said it. So—you ready to run through it?"

Zeni lifted her eyes to Trey's dark gaze while the first shock of discovery faded from her system. That process was aided by the irony mixed with challenge in his voice. He didn't think she'd do it.

A second before, she might not have. Now, she wavered. "I—can see why this scene is pivotal to the story."

"Being such a turn on?"

"No, not so much that." Her answer was for what he'd said rather than the condemnation in his voice. "It's the moment when the protagonist realizes he prefers an aggressive woman."

Trey grunted. "That's one way of putting it."

"I'm just saying I see the point," she insisted.

"You don't mind giving it a try then?"

The quiet note of a dare was in his voice. How could she not answer it?

She glanced at the script page again, as if trying to decide, but actually to commit the lines to memory. Tossing it aside, she rose to her feet in abrupt readiness. Anger was one way to root out embarrassment and gain an edge.

"Sir infidel," she said clearly, as she paced toward him in assumed grandeur. "What brings you to me?"

"Curiosity," he answered in his turn. "I wanted to see what a warrior queen looks like."

"You dare much. Do you not know you could lose your head if found here?" She circled him, putting out a hand to run it across his shoulder and down the flinching muscles of his back. Keeping her fingertips upon him as she continued around in front of him again, she let them rest above his heart.

He had definitely read the scene; his heartbeat drummed against her palm and something that might almost be anticipation leapt in his eyes. "I did not know," he said, "but it might be worth the risk."

"From where do you come?" She eased closer, rising on tiptoe as if about to collect a kiss.

His head dipped toward her in a way that didn't seem entirely an act. "Another time, another place."

With a slow, lingering movement she smoothed her hand downward; over the flat surface of his abdomen to his lower belly. Quite gently, she tested the heat and rock hardness of him. "As you are a stranger who may not see the dawn, I would have you."

He swallowed, and she felt a definite springing lift under her hand. It was thrilling to know she could affect him that way. The exhilaration was so great she almost forgot this was an act, almost curled her fingers around him. Or perhaps she did, for his voice was hoarse as he made the scripted answer.

"And I you."

"Prepare for it then," she said in tones of command, and used both hands to push him toward the sofa.

He didn't resist at all, though he pretended to stumble as the script instructed before falling backward upon the cushions. She was upon him at once, straddling him, dragging his shirt open with the popping of buttons. He rose against the hot core of her in a way that made her gasp low in her throat. A moment later, she felt his hands slide under the raised hem of her caftan, pressing with urgent fingertips, testing the smooth surface of her skin and the muscles underneath.

She bent lower to take his face in her hands and match

her open mouth to his as if it was her right and privilege as the queen whom none could or would deny. She plumbed the moist depths, swirling her tongue to receive his very essence, licking the slick underside of his tongue. She wanted to take him into her body and make him hers.

Hers alone. Hers always.

He gripped the curves of her hips, grinding against her. She was melting inside and burning up outside, while the scent of their arousal surrounded them, a blending of sweet peas and patchouli and the spice of his aftershave.

She reached for his belt buckle, pulling it open. Releasing its pin, she flipped the ends aside and made short work of the button of his jeans. As the zipper gaped she felt silky cotton briefs and hot male.

It was then that Midnight yowled and leaped from the cushion above them. His small feet thumped into Zeni's back before the kitten launched himself onto the chest that sat before the sofa and then down to the floor.

Trey stilled in place for endless seconds. With an abrupt bunching of muscles, then, he heaved over, taking Zeni with him over the edge of the sofa cushions. He thrust out his forearm in time to break their fall, cradling her with his other arm as they settled to the sisal rug, trapped between coffee table and sofa. She moaned in protest as she lost direct contact with his mouth, his heat and power.

"Cut?" His breathing was fast, deep and difficult as he made that husky, movie filming suggestion.

She gazed up at him, half-stunned and bereft at the withdrawal of something that had seemed right and inevitable, something that had nothing whatever to do with a movie, a pretend engagement, or lines written for other people and for other reasons.

What did it matter who he was or what she was not. She didn't expect promises, didn't need them. All she wanted was this moment, with its upheaval of emotions and closeness of skin to skin and mouth to mouth in a physical welding that was as nature meant it to be, the way nature demanded.

"No," she said, and wound her legs around his as she slid an arm to the back of his neck, holding him to her. "The scene doesn't end here. I want you, just you."

"Ah, Zeni," he said against her hair. "I thought you said you were bashful."

"Sometimes. Not now." The words were choked, barely a whisper.

"Thank God for it."

Within seconds, the robe-like caftan was stripped away over her head and her bikini panties, his jeans and shorts were gone. He paused to retrieve a condom from his wallet, but for nothing else. Pulling down the front of her bra, he allowed the stretchy fabric to frame and lift her breasts for his attention, but the rest of her was gloriously naked to his probing touch, his licking, suckling invasion.

He was thorough, unhurried, though alive to her soft inhalations, her clutching hands, her flexing knees and soft pleas. And when she was hot, wet, and trembling on the edge of desperation, he gave her surcease, tumultuous and slow, powerful and fine. He gave her exactly what she asked for; he gave her himself.

Zeni held him while their hearts slowed and breathing became even again. He supported his weight on one elbow while brushing the hair away from her face, but did not withdraw. She would have rug burns from the sisal in the morning, she knew, but he would have them on his knees; it seemed a rough equality.

She thought of instigating a move to her bed, but was afraid he might take it as a signal to go. She didn't want that. Not yet.

She touched a finger to his ear, following its whorl before trailing it along his jaw to the center of his chin. Reversing that path, she explored the strong line of his neck and across to his shoulder where she carefully traced his tattoo, outlining the roses and their thorns.

He glanced at what she was doing from the corners of his eyes, and a smile grooved the planes of his face. "That reminds me, though I'm not sure just why—I have something of yours. "

"You do?"

Her voice sounded languorous with contentment, totally lacking in interest. That wasn't far from wrong.

He reached for his jeans and delved into the pocket, bringing out something small that gleamed briefly between his fingers. With great care, then, he gave it a twist to open its locking mechanism and touched it to her nostril.

It was her small gold nose ring. He was threading it carefully into the hole made for it. She could feel it moving, delicately gliding into the place it belonged.

The operation was no doubt a first for him, yet he was as competent at it as he was most things. She didn't move as he turned the ring as it should be and then fastened its closure, yet she felt the most incredible giving sensation at her very center.

Something about the intimacy of that small incursion into her body affected him as well; she felt him harden again inside her, expanding to fill her with amazing completeness. She tightened internal muscles around him in a deep caress. He drew in a startled breath.

And abruptly they were swept up again, striving toward the ultimate pleasure, the joining of hearts and minds as well as bodies, which was life's gift, and its best recompense for the punishment of being born human and aware that it was not infinite.

Sometime later, Trey eased from her and rose, padding to the bathroom to be rid of the condom. Afterward, he picked her up, stripped away the constriction of her bra and carried her to bed. Flinging back the sheet and blanket, he sat down with her in his lap, then lay back and drew her close against him while lofting the covers back over them both.

Midnight leaped up to join them, winding his small, lithe shape into a circle before settling into the curve of Zeni's body. He purred all three of them to sleep.

It was barely three a.m. when Trey roused, yawned, and slipped from the bed. Leaning down, he tucked the sheet and blanket back in around her.

"Where are you going?" she murmured, still half-asleep.

"Home, before all of Chamelot figures out I didn't sleep there."

"I don't care what they think."

His voice held warm amusement as he answered. "I guess I'll have to care for both of us. But Zeni—"

Something in his voice brought her closer to being awake. She raised on one elbow and propped her head on the heel of her hand. "Yes?"

"I am not going to be in that scene with you."

What was he telling her? That he didn't intend to rehearse with her again? Or that he wouldn't be returning, wouldn't make love to her again? "You mean—"

"I'm sorry, but I can't do it. Or maybe I should say I won't do it."

"Why not?" The words were stark, edged with sudden pain.

"I can't stand there while Peabody says the words I said last night, has make-believe sex with you in front of the cameras and crew and whoever else may crowd onto the set."

She let out the breath she had not known she was holding. "You mean you won't be Zenobia's guard."

Trey straightened and walked to the door where he turned back for an instant. "Peabody knew what was in the script. The idea of having the man who showed up to support you stand and watch it as a palace guard was his idea of a snide joke, a trick to make him—me—feel foolish. The man is an arrogant asshole. You can do what you like, but I'm not playing his game."

He didn't wait for her answer. Stepping from the bedroom, he closed the door behind him. The click as it shut was quiet but definite.

CHAPTER TEN

irst time for everything, and all that, but Trey had never been seduced before. That it had happened with Zeni was unbelievable. He stopped dead-still every now and then over the next couple of days, staring at nothing, stunned into immobility by the memory. He caught himself smiling at nothing while rubbing away the heat that flared on the back of his neck. His flashbacks were hot; his showers cold.

It took about the same amount of time to realize Zeni was avoiding him. She couldn't do that completely, of course; they saw each other as usual at the Watering Hole and spoke of this and that, mostly business. She didn't linger, however, and barely met his eyes. There were no more suggestions that he help with her lines, no invitation to come up to her apartment.

Was she embarrassed, or was she mad because he would

not be doing the dream sequence with her? He wished he knew.

The fact was, he was more than a little pissed off himself. He'd half expected her to say she wouldn't be doing that sexy scene with Derek after all. She hadn't done that, which meant he was forced to imagine her as an aggressive, love-starved Zenobia to the actor's horny quarterback. That didn't exactly improve his temper.

It might be that Zeni had been disappointed in the way he made love, but who could tell? Women were better at keeping these things hidden than men. Or she could have decided it would be best if they didn't carry matters any further. If that was it, it appeared he was going to be the last to know.

He could ask her but it was doubtful he would get a straight answer. She was an expert at avoiding questions. He'd think he had her attention, but then she was busy somewhere else and he was left talking to thin air.

The long and short of it was, he was frustrated, and in more ways than one.

He was working on his bike at the arena in late afternoon of the second day, when the sheriff came by. Strolling toward him, Lance asked, "What's up?"

"Getting ready for a run-through of the ring tournament scene, a sort of dress rehearsal."

"You got it all figured out, right? Nobody's going to get hurt?"

"More or less. Which one of us is going to win is not in the script, so that's up for grabs." Trey gave him a tight grin.

"Literally."

Lance snorted. "Yeah, I get it, grabbing the ring and all that. I just hope you guys know what you're doing."

Trey took no offense; it was his cousin's job as sheriff to see that no one got hurt. The two of them shot the bull for a minute or so before he found an opening to ask the question that was on his mind.

"Tell me something. Does Mandy ever, well, make you an offer she won't let you refuse? I mean, in the bedroom?"

Lance gave him a hard look. "None of your business, cuz."

"I'm not intending to get into your personal life. It's just that there's this situation."

"What situation would that be?"

Trey concentrated on tightening the nut under his wrench. "A woman initiating sex doesn't bother me, and a woman on top works just fine any time, but what does it mean when one comes on strong with no warning?"

"Maybe that she likes you?" The sheriff looked as if he wanted to laugh, but was waiting for the punch line.

"I'm serious here."

"Could be she thinks you weren't moving fast enough."

"I don't think so. Not unless I've lost all knack for reading the signals."

"It happens, especially when it's important. But what's the big deal? Everything turned out okay, right?"

Against his will, Trey's brain handed him another fast and graphic replay of that night. "More than okay. Only— how do you know when it's real and not an act? How can you tell when you are what's turning her on, and not what's going on in her head?"

"You don't."

"Not ever?" Trey was sorely disappointed. He'd expected better from a man who had been living with a wife for well over a year.

Lance gave him a quick look from under his brows. "One thing might be whether her eyes are open or closed, if she's looking at you or not. But it's not foolproof. She could be concentrating on how you're making her feel."

"That helps just bunches."

"Yeah, well, you're supposed to be engaged, so I don't know what you're doing out with this needy female. That is unless she's—"

"Never mind," Trey interrupted. "I'm sorry I asked." He suddenly saw where Lance was coming from with his not wanting to go into his personal life with Mandy. He didn't much want to talk particulars about Zeni and what had happened between them, either.

"Just as well." Lance nodded toward the other bike club members at the upper end of the arena. "Looks like this dress rehearsal is about to get underway."

He was right. Jake, their cousin from over near Turn-Coupe, was fitting an antique-looking knight's helmet over his head while astride his rumbling Harley—trust a Benedict to always be out front. With it settled into place, Jake took the long lance that was handed to him, revved up his bike and began a fast circuit around the arena.

Trey got to his feet, squinting against the bright sunlight

as he watched the action. "Where did the armor come from? We've been waiting for it to be delivered."

"Guess it showed up." Lance watched the rider for a second as well, before he went on. "Peabody's personal assistant, or whatever she is, was out front when I got here just now. She was checking a list while a couple of guys unloaded a van."

"The movie folks seem to be on the ball with the tournament. We churned up the ground here in the arena floor pretty good after the rain the other night. Somebody from the company brought in equipment and smoothed it out again. It was nice and even when we got here this morning."

"Getting it ready for the filming, maybe?"

Trey tipped his head in assent. "In a couple of days, if this rehearsal with armor goes as it should. The stuff may take some getting used to, though." Privately, he thought the ruts made today might need leveling again before they brought in any cameras, which made the work done the night before a waste of effort. He wasn't complaining, however, as it was on the movie company's dime.

"Probably not metal, but plastic or some composite material, don't you think?" Lance took his sunglasses from a pocket and slipped them on as he tracked their cousin's progress. "But the lance he's holding looks to be painted wood."

Trey barely heard him over the roar as Jake whipped past again, trailing a cloud of dust. "Both dangerous in a crash then."

Lance pivoted on one heel as he tracked Jake's progress.

"Looks like he's going for it at the end of this round."

"It does."

Trey could barely hear his own answer as Jake flew past where he and Lance stood once more. Engine roaring like a jet plane on takeoff, their cousin made a wide turn and then sped straight down the track laid out as an approach to the series of rings dangling from the archway which had been moved to the arena's center point to prevent hitting the end wall. The idea was to catch one of the rings on the lance. If the thing came loose as it should, then Jake could carry it away with him. If not, he was supposed to drop the lance before he could be dragged off his bike.

The sun gleamed on the rider's make-believe armor, slid along the blue and white painted wood of the lance Jake clamped under his right arm, and flashed over the chrome of his bike. Wind from his passage fluttered the plume that sprang from the top of his helmet. The dust that rolled upward in his wake was like a cloud of powdered gold. His spinning tires left a plowed furrow in the soft ground. The noise was incredible, drowning out the cry of a hawk from overhead and the buzz of a wasp not two feet from Trey's face.

Everyone in the arena stopped what they were doing to watch. No one spoke; the very air shuddered with the grumbling power of the bike hurtling down the track that led to the rings.

A weird sense of something not quite right swept over Trey. It felt like the time he nearly stepped out of his boat onto a cottonmouth moccasin, or the one when he stopped at an intersection when the light was green, and narrowly missed being hit by an eighteen-wheeler running the red.

He took a step forward. Then he plunged into a run with a shout rising in his throat, though why he was yelling and what he meant to say he had no idea.

Jake never heard him. His front tire hit something under the dirt and reared up like a wild stallion. Jake dropped the lance and snatched for the right handgrip, but was too late. The front wheel wrenched around, spilling Jake off. Then the heavy motorcycle crashed down inches from his legs.

Trey sprinted toward the wreck. Lance was right beside him, and the rest of the bike club not far behind. They arrived in a jostling group, yelling, shouting, spouting questions and advice, none of it very helpful.

Dropping to one knee beside Jake, Trey cursed the knight's helmet that might be photographic as all hell but offered no protection compared to a biker's helmet. As gently as possible, he slid the tin can from his cousin's head, taking care not to shift the position of his neck.

Jake's eyes were closed, his face pale, his hair matted with sweat. He seemed to be barely breathing.

"Jake, buddy. Talk to me. Tell me where it hurts."

There was no answer.

Lance, who had dropped to his knees across from Trey, sprang up and took out his cell phone. As he turned away, he punched in the emergency code.

Trey felt for a pulse at the carotid artery in Jake's neck. It was there, but seemed weak. Quickly, he ran his hands

over his cousin's lax arms and legs as he'd seen Beau do so
many times as an EMT. They seemed okay. Gingerly, he
began to probe Jake's scalp, reaching down under his neck
on both sides to test the back of his head.

His questing fingers ran into the warm wetness of blood,
enough that he felt his heart shrink. But that was not all.
Beneath it was something hard. A careful brushing of the
sand around it exposed a length of wood. It appeared to be a
2 x 6 board set on edge and with the dirt then pounded hard
to set it. A third or so of its width had been left unburied,
but camouflaged with loosely packed earth.

Jake's bike had hit it and rebounded, throwing its rider
backward onto the hard edge as he fell.

It was a booby trap, and it was Jake's misfortune that
he'd been the one to spring it.

Trey lifted his head, his gaze bleak as he met Lance's
eyes where he had come to stand over him. They shared the
same conclusion, unspoken but obvious.

Jake should not have been the first rider to try the stunt.
As president and leader of the club, that duty was Trey's.

The booby trap was meant for him. It should have been
him lying silent and defenseless in the dirt.

CHAPTER ELEVEN

*J*t was later, much later, when Trey reached the Watering Hole. The place was closed of course, but a light still glowed upstairs in Zeni's apartment. He let himself in at the back with his key and made his way through the storeroom and into the front with its familiar obstacle course of tables and chairs. He didn't turn on the lights; he didn't need them, for one thing, but he also didn't want some concerned citizen noticing through the window and banging on the door, maybe asking for news of Jake.

Sustenance was his purpose, and he moved around behind the counter to the refrigerator that sat beneath it. He'd just come from the hospital in New Orleans. They had a cafeteria there, but it was closed by the time he realized he was hungry. A plain ham sandwich, tall glass of milk, and a piece of Zeni's coconut pie were what he needed now, and the sooner the better.

He knew when she started downstairs because the staircase light came on. He'd figured she would come down, which was another reason he'd stopped instead of going home—or to the house he called by that name. He'd called to tell her what happened, but she'd want the details.

That was probably all she'd want, but it didn't much matter. Information in exchange for a sight of her in the white robe-like thing she'd worn before, one that skimmed her curves but left plenty of room for imagination, would be a fair exchange.

"I thought I heard you down here," she said as she came around the corner.

"Who else?" He didn't look up as he was carefully transferring two pieces of pie to a plate at one time.

"Right. You're the only thief who raids the refrigerator instead of the cash register."

"And a good thing to, since you don't have even a baseball bat with you for protection."

He paused to enjoy the view as she stood with the light behind her, outlining her curves with indelible precision. He stored the memory away with care, figuring he might like to bring it out now and then for, oh, the next hundred years or so.

"The last thing I'd need against you."

"I don't know so much about that," he muttered as he reached for a carton of milk and tore open the top.

"What?"

"Nothing."

The look she gave him held dark suspicion, but she let the comment pass. "How is Jake?"

"He's okay." He folded a slice of ham into a piece of bread and wolfed down a big bite, chasing it with milk before he went on. "Poor guy will have to wear a neck brace for a while, and can't ride in the tournament. But he'll be good to go in a month or two."

"A neck brace?"

"Cracked vertebrae." He finished his half sandwich. "He was damn lucky he wasn't paralyzed. A few inches lower—" He shook his head.

"People have been saying that it should've been you." She walked closer, maybe to see his face in the dim light of the neon window signs advertising beer, soft drinks, and various other tipples and edibles.

"Could be, who knows." Trey didn't intend to make a lot of the possibility, not until he and Lance figured out who was behind this supposed accident.

"They also say that board he hit was planted. Who would do such a thing?"

So much for keeping that part quiet. "Maybe it was, maybe it wasn't. We don't know for sure." He started working on the pie.

"If it was, I can't imagine how they hoped to get away with it," she said with a frown. "I mean the board was right there. Did they think no one would notice?"

"The thing could've been left behind from some old rodeo event or repair project. At least, the culprit probably depended on people thinking that."

Her face was tinted with blue and red from the signs, while her eyes glistened with a dozen colors. "What matters is that it was there, and was probably meant for you to hit. You might have been killed."

"I didn't and I wasn't."

She shook her head so her hair that drifted around her shoulders gleamed with colors as well, more fascinating than the dyes she affected so often. The need to touch those rainbow strands, to run his fingers through them, was so strong Trey curled his fingers around his fork until the handle almost cut into his palm.

"It could happen," she said. "One minute people can be living, breathing, working, going about their lives without a thought, and the next they are just gone."

She was really upset; he could tell from the quiver in her voice more than from what she said. Finishing the pie, he put his plate in the sink. He tossed the empty milk carton into the trash before he turned to her. Trying for a light note, he said, "Hey, don't count me out. I have fight left in me yet."

Tears appeared in her eyes, gleaming in the semi darkness. He stepped from behind the counter and eased next to her. Using his thumbs, he brushed away the moisture that had gathered in the hollows under her eyes. She turned away for an instant, but then swung back suddenly and came into his arms. He folded her close, uncertain if he was worthy of her trust, much less the task of soothing her fear.

"Ah, Zeni," he whispered against her hair. "Don't cry."

"I was so worried," she said her breath warm against his

neck. "Everyone was so sure at first that it was you who had been hurt. But then they said it was Jake. I felt so guilty at the relief, because I was glad—glad it was him, not you."

"Don't worry about it," he said quietly against the top of her head. "It's a natural reaction, being glad someone you know missed being hurt."

She was so very soft and warm, the smooth resilience of her a tender enticement. The heat and shape of her that fit so well against his body sent such need arcing through him that he nearly groaned with it. On so many occasions—too many—he had imagined boosting her onto one of the Watering Hole's tables. Once he had her there, he'd pictured skimming up under the short jean skirt she usually wore to touch and hold what lay underneath. He'd step between her spread legs and she'd clamp them around him, and then—

He'd tried so hard to keep a decent employer and employee relationship between them, to accept that she wanted nothing more and pretend he felt the same. He'd sparred with her, exchanged barbs and honey coated insults with her, and enjoyed every second while knowing it was a perverse form of courtship.

He'd allowed her to run the Watering Hole and his life, up to a point, in the half-acknowledged hope she might realize it could become a full-time job. She hadn't taken the bait, and he wasn't sure she ever would. He had the feeling she might be gone one day, drifting away from Chamelot like the dandelions of the tattoo on her back, going who knows where, seeking the answer that was blowing in the wind.

Prickly yet tenderhearted, sarcastic but concerned; she was everything he'd ever wanted or needed. Why she'd avoided him since the rainy night she'd taken him on as Zenobia he couldn't say, but his heart clamored inside him with the need to see that it didn't happen now.

The taste he'd had of her then merely whetted his lust for more instead of satisfying it. The days of being unable to touch her, to hold her, raised his need to an unbearable ache. These things coalesced in his mind, pushing at him until fantasy turned into reality. One moment he was holding her with no thought of anything beyond comfort and reassurance, and the next they were mouth to mouth and he was lifting her onto the table behind her.

She stiffened, pulling away from him. "What are you doing?"

Something I thought about so many times—you've no idea how many."

"Getting it on standing up?"

"Getting you on top of a table, here where I've watched you moving back and forth, day after day." He smoothed his hands up and down her back, easing them to her hips in an orgy of touch, before sliding them along her thighs. His every sense was alive to the realization that she wore nothing under her robe except some kind of silky slip of a nightgown.

"You mean—"

She seemed to lose whatever thought she might have had as he leaned to taste the skin of her neck, running his tongue down its curve. He smiled against the enticing spot where her neck joined her shoulder, not from ego satisfaction but from sheer joy that he was able to distract her. With that, in spite of his disclaimer, ran the exultation of being alive and well when he could just as easily be lying in a hospital bed or dead.

"I do mean," he said against her skin.

"With me, not just any female in an apron?"

She was gripping his tattooed shoulder with one hand while rubbing the other over his chest, each small pass sending waves of fire over him. "Only you," he said, the words so low he wasn't sure she could hear them. "No other."

"You're not such a bad boy then," she murmured, bringing her hand up to plow her fingers through his hair.

"Who said I might be?" Not that he cared about that; he only asked so she might not notice the slide of his fingers under the raised hem of her robe.

"The girls who come in here," she said a little breathlessly, "teenagers impressed with your daredevil ways, your biker club and tattoos."

"One tattoo."

"Really? None here?" She shifted her hand from his shoulder to his back, and then down to grasp the curve of his backside. "Or here?"

"You should know better."

"Except I don't remember noticing the back so much as the front."

"Zeni—"

158 | JENNIFER BLAKE

It was a groan. Sometimes imagination could be painful.
"I think you need to see just how good I can be."

"Or how bad?" she asked on a gasp as he put his hands
on her knees and spread them apart.

He showed her instead of answering, pulling her gently
rounded bottom to the edge of the table and pushing her
back until she lay down. Then he dropped to his knees.

She was succulent and delicious, tart yet sweet, as heady
as some fruit-flavored liqueur with a mind-bending hint of
coconut pie. He enjoyed her in slow indulgence, probing
with his tongue, applying suction, biting gently. He brought
his fingers into play until she moaned with a musical sound
of need and the pulsation of internal muscles. She writhed
in extremity and escalating fervor until she cried his name
and her thighs quivered as she fought his grip. And when
that paroxysm began to fade, she pushed up, reaching for
him as he stood, releasing his belt and zipper while he
stripped away her nightclothes and then retrieved the
condom he'd replaced in his wallet days ago.

She took it from him and sheathed him with shaking
fingers. Then she drew him between her legs and guided
him home. She dragged him closer with both hands while
inhaling so deep that the warm surfaces of her breasts
surged against his chest. Yes, and then flattened against it
as he sank deeper still.

And it was every bit as miraculous as he'd expected. It
was purest surging magic that he fed by laying her back
again, watching the play of neon light in red blue and green
on her breasts, her belly and thighs, watching her face as he

touched her, took possession of her with fast, jarring thrusts. And she watched him, her lips parted and swollen as she panted for breath, her face flushed and beautiful, holding his eyes with her own.

That was until she convulsed around him, until he pumped a final time before bending protectively over her. She let her lashes fall then, shutting him out.

CHAPTER TWELVE

*O*ne corner of the big exhibit building being used by the movie company for reception and registration had been set up as a cantina. Zeni's arrival there had a two-fold purpose. She'd delivered warming trays of biscuits stuffed with sausage or ham, and open trays of doughnuts, muffins or homemade granola bars, setting them out on the serving table next to the industrial sized coffee and juice machines provided by the Watering Hole. Then she sat down to wait for her early morning appointment that Derek had set up the day before.

He was nowhere in sight, but she didn't mind; it was good to be off her feet for a few minutes. She'd been up for hours, baking for the movie crew as well as for her usual customers. The last pans of biscuits had still been in the oven when she left, though Gloria had arrived to see they came out on time and to make any special breakfast orders from the retirees who congregated every morning at daybreak.

Gloria could handle it just fine, Zeni knew, but she still hoped the run-through of the dream sequence wouldn't take long. She usually caught up with her paperwork between the breakfast and lunch rush hours on Gloria's eight-hour shift days. If she didn't get back to it fairly soon she'd be working late tonight, as well as getting up early again in the morning.

Just the thought of it was enough to make her yawn, though sleeplessness the night before could have had something to do with it. She might as well not have gone to bed, for all the good it did her. She'd lain awake for hours, thinking, wondering and remembering. Heat rose in her face and the blood fizzed in her veins, even now, as she thought of the use Trey had found for one of the coffee shop tables.

Never in her life had she felt anything that came close to the moments they'd shared. The closeness in her apartment had been a revelation, but the encounter on a table in the dark had changed her in some way she couldn't quite understand. That he'd wanted her as she wanted him, that he'd needed her so desperately he would risk public exposure, had sent her soaring.

She'd thought she wanted nothing from Trey if she couldn't have it all. She was wrong.

She wanted whatever she might be allowed from this mock engagement, all the sweet joy and passion that she'd found in his arms and might again, however fleetingly. At the same time, she felt a profound connection of mind and soul to him, as if he'd somehow become half her whole.

It was that last which made her toss and turn. She couldn't see how this was going to turn out, feared the physical accord between them could never lead to anything more. If it ended when the movie was done, she wasn't sure she could stay in Chamelot. As painful as it might be, she would have to go.

She'd done that after her mother died, simply walked away and left everything behind—the apartment in the old house they'd shared, their ratty furniture, most of her clothes, the degrees and job prospects she'd earned as a prodigy. Over a period of four or five years she'd slowly worked her way upriver, but diverted to investigate Chamelot for no reason other than she liked the name. Staying had never been in the plan. After her car died on her, she'd intended to work long enough to get it fixed then move on. Somehow, it hadn't happened that way.

She'd started over once before with nothing except hope and a willingness to work. She could do it again if she had to, surely she could.

Oh, but she wouldn't be completely alone. No way could she leave Midnight behind, now that he was a part of her life. She certainly couldn't take him back to where she'd found him; it would be too much like abandoning him, as her mother, however unwillingly, had abandoned her.

No, the two of them could hit the road and just keep going.

The only problem was that she hadn't known before what was missing from her life: this sleepy little river town and its warm and friendly people, the coffee shop and its regulars, the man who owned it and the tenuous yet heart-satisfying connection between them. Now she did.

The sharp click of stilettos on the building's concrete floor snapped her out of her reverie. She looked around to see Bettina, Derek's tall blonde assistant, bearing down on her. She was almost glad to see her, since it was possible she was coming to tell her the rehearsal was called off.

"First you were late, and now you're early," the woman said with glacial annoyance. "It would be helpful if you could at least be consistent."

All right, so she wasn't glad to see her. "I don't believe the crew would consider it too helpful if I was consistently late with their breakfast."

"I see. If you had told me you would be bringing it when I called, I might have arranged something so you didn't sit here in the way."

She was hardly in the way, since half the tables around her were empty. Zeni arched a brow and waited to see what the assistant wanted. It wasn't long in coming.

"Before you see Derek, I need to lay out a few ground rules." Bettina pulled out a chair and perched on the edge of it as if she had no time to waste.

Zeni was willing to allow that the woman was probably doing her job; still, her attitude was beyond irritating. "Rules for what?"

"Your relationship with Derek. It will be to your advantage if you cooperate fully in whatever he asks of you."

"No doubt, since he's the director."

Bettina narrowed her eyes. "That isn't what I meant. Most women who work—closely—with him are thrilled with the experience, and find him to be very generous when their time together is over. It can be a positive career move, as well as a pleasurable one."

"Are you saying—" Zeni was afraid she knew, but needed to be certain.

"Don't be stupid. Derek is a sensual man and an excellent actor who prefers a high degree of realism in his scenes. It gives him an edge, one that translates well to the screen."

"In other words, he gets a charge out of making it with the women who are cast opposite him, even the bit players." Zeni had grown used to plain speaking in her exchanges with Trey. It came in handy now.

"If you want to put it that way."

"And you would be familiar with this method of his firsthand, having worked with him in television?"

Bettina's smile was a mere lifting of her upper lip. "I've probably benefited more than anyone else, though you must realize the intimate association between Derek and myself did not end when *Rifle Fire* was finally canceled."

"The two of you are still a couple then." That was certainly what the rumor mill had said, though Zeni had wondered after her costume meeting with Derek.

"Naturally."

"And yet—"

The look Bettina gave her was pitying. "We have an open arrangement, with sex as one of many benefits. We are partners, and the film we are making is of paramount importance to both of us. As Derek's personal assistant, it's my job to see that he has whatever he needs to do his best work."

Zeni's laugh held an element of disbelief. "Some job."

"You can say whatever you like," Bettina told her with chilly hauteur, "as long as you give him whatever he likes."

"I don't believe I can do—"

Bettina held up a hand to interrupt as she glanced toward the building's open doorway. "Here comes Derek now. Remember what I've told you." As she got to her feet she added, "Your boyfriend called to say we should find someone else to play his part. Under the circumstances, that was probably a wise decision."

"My fiancé," Zeni corrected, and was glad beyond words that she had that claim on Trey, at least for now.

"Are you talking about Benedict?" Derek asked as he joined them. "Such a shame that he's bowing out, but I'm sure we can work around it."

"I'll leave you to get on with it," Bettina said.

Derek gave her an absent nod. If he noticed the intimate little smile she sent him before walking away, it wasn't apparent. Nor was there any sign that he knew how Bettina had been attempting to smooth the way toward his next conquest. That last was the only reason Zeni was able to remain at the table with him when he took the chair his special assistant had been using.

"Finding another man to take Trey's place shouldn't be a problem," Zeni suggested, thinking another warm body present during the rehearsal sounded like an excellent idea. "I mean, all he has to do is stand there."

Derek's smile was brief. "But the part isn't at all necessary."

It seemed Trey could be right, that adding him to the scene had been a petty attempt at payback, if not a rather snide joke. She hadn't blamed Trey for opting out of it before; now she was actively glad.

She wished she'd never agreed to play Zenobia; she wouldn't have if she'd seen the script ahead of time. And she would refuse the part this minute if she didn't have such a strong sense of responsibility.

Letting people down was something she avoided at all costs. That was a reaction from childhood, she knew. Her mother had been artistic, charming, charismatic, and beloved by all, but it was a mistake to depend on her. A promise to her had been only a possibility; nothing was certain until it happened. Disappointments without number—birthday parties that never happened, permission slips never signed, shopping trips that never took, school programs and graduations never attended—had made Zeni her complete opposite.

"It might not be necessary," she said with a tight smile, "but another character of some kind might add interest."

"You have a specific role in mind, maybe a hand-maiden?" Derek asked, sitting back in his chair.

That had not been Zeni's first thought, but it would do. "Sounds reasonable for the time and place."

"On second thought, forget it. Putting out another call for such a minor part would be ridiculous."

"I could probably recruit someone." Gloria was a possibility, though Zeni knew she would have to talk her helper at the Watering Hole into the role. Regardless, a handmaiden, even in exotic dress, might be too much like a maid for her to stomach.

"I'll think about it. Meanwhile—"

He paused as the cleaner who had just finished clearing the nearest table came toward them. A rather plain girl with nondescript features and dishwater blonde hair, she halted beside Derek with a half-filled trash bag in one hand and a wet cloth in the other. The frown he turned on her warned against interruption, but she seemed oblivious.

"Excuse me, Mr. Peabody, but I couldn't help overhearing," she said, her voice breathless and eyes pleading. "I could be a handmaiden if you need one. I was in our school play last year, and I—"

"No," he said in icy rejection, his features set and mouth turned down at the corners. "You aren't the right type."

"Oh, but if you'd only give me a chance!"

"I said no. Get on with your job."

"I—yes. Yes, sir." The girl's face turned red in blotches and tears spilled over her eyelids. She backed away half a dozen steps. Turning, she ran toward the makeshift kitchen area.

Zeni watched the girl's flight in helpless sympathy before turning to Derek. "Was it necessary to be so rude?"

"It was, yes. Otherwise she'd have stood there for ages, yammering on and on about her part in this ridiculous school play as if that gave her some kind of experience. She was a dog. Even if I wanted a handmaiden, I'd never choose her."

"I can't see that she has to be especially attractive for such an unimportant part."

"You wouldn't, since you aren't in the business." His lips curled at one corner. "She needs to be decorative for this dream sequence in particular and the movie in general. More than that, I like the people around me to be attractive, even if they can't all be as beautiful as you."

"If that is supposed to make me feel grateful for being chosen, I can't say it does."

His face took on a pained look. "You aren't one of those women's libbers, are you?"

"I don't have to be an advocate for women's liberation to feel for another female. That girl just wanted a hearing."

"Sorry, but all women aren't born equal, my darling Zeni. Some start out ahead of the game, genetically more attractive to the males of the species."

She was no doubt supposed to be flattered. Instead, she was disgusted by the blatant egocentricity. It seemed all females in Derek's movies were chosen for their suitability as his bed partners, with talent being optional. And what did that say about his selection of her?

It had been no slip of the tongue, it seemed, when he called her *his* Zenobia.

"Enough of this," he said in brisk dismissal, as if destroying someone's hopes was less than nothing. "You read the script, correct? What did you think of the dream sequence? Ready to give it a run-through?"

"Now?" She glanced around at the people occupying the surrounding tables.

"Not here, of course. Some place where we will have the necessary privacy. Perhaps my motor home?"

Derek's smile was too expectant, too certain she must feel the same anticipation that he did.

He was deluded. "Certainly not."

"Not that I'd object," he said, his expression verging on the lascivious. "Tables can have their uses during—intimate—rehearsals, as can desks and sofas."

She could feel a flush creeping up her chest and neck to her cheekbones, one brought on by anger and remembrance. The vivid images in her head that involved a table had nothing to do with the director and everything to do with a certain biker with strong thigh muscles.

"I do object," she answered in clipped tones. "That scene isn't—well, I'm not comfortable with it."

"But it's an act."

"Even so."

"The set will be closed if that's the way you want it. But the pretense is nothing that hasn't been done a thousand times over in the past few decades. It's supposed to be hot. As I told you before—"

"I remember. It's a football player's wet dream, and all that. Regardless, I'd still like to see it toned down."

His tolerant air turned into petulance. "Playing prude again, I see."

The way she had played that scene with Trey came unbidden to her mind. She'd been far from a prude then.

Not that she had any intention of duplicating the action with Derek.

"I'm not at all prudish in private. In public is something else again. Is there nothing that can be done with the scene?"

His bottom lip protruded another quarter of an inch and he crossed his arms over his chest. "I don't think so. It was written to create a particular effect. Changing it could change the whole dynamic of the movie."

"Oh, come on. It can't be that important."

He looked stunned, as if it'd been so long since someone called him on one of his pronouncements that he couldn't believe it was happening. "I assure you it is. I like you as Zenobia, but you aren't irreplaceable, darling Zeni. Either you play the part the way it's written, including every action, or you don't play it at all."

He thought he had her. The triumph he expected from his ultimatum colored his voice.

He was wrong.

"Not a problem." She rose to her feet. "I'm sure you can find another Zenobia." She turned away, picking up her shoulder bag that hung from the back of her chair.

Derek lunged from his seat, catching her wrist in a hard grip as his face turned an ugly red. "Hold on. We aren't finished here."

"I believe we are." She rotated her wrist, twisting her arm free.

"Sit down, Zeni darling. That is, unless you would like me to have a talk with Benedict about the man who was your father."

She couldn't move for long seconds, could scarcely breathe. The threat was so far from anything she'd thought he might say that she couldn't think.

"Sit back down. Now."

Returning to her chair was one of the hardest things Zeni had ever done. Yet to refuse was impossible. Hard, biting words echoed in her mind, words that would tear Derek's ego and character to shreds, but she swallowed them down.

"What do you know of my father?" She demanded in a hoarse whisper.

"Did it never occur to you that I might have you investigated? I had big plans for you, but nasty little surprises that might ruin my investment of time and money were no part of them."

She looked at him with loathing. "I don't know what you think you've discovered, but my own mother couldn't name my father."

He gave a snide laugh. "Couldn't? Or wouldn't?"

Zeni felt cold and sick inside. She'd known the truth—or as much of it as she had guessed, might have to come out— but thought she could put it off. She should've known better. "So you're saying I'm no longer a suitable investment? Too bad."

"I'm not saying that at all. The only thing that's changed is the spin that may be required for your life story." He shrugged with elaborate unconcern. "Plus how grateful you will need to be, and when I'll expect you to express it."

"What makes you think Trey doesn't know everything already?"

He gave a slow shake of his head. "If you'd told him, you wouldn't be sitting here now. No, my dearest Zeni. You haven't said a word. You can't, because you're afraid of what his reaction will be."

The creep was right, though it was also true there had been no pressing reason to explain before Derek and his movie company appeared in Chamelot. Everything had been fine until then.

She ached with the mass of pain and anger, despair and hatred inside her. She'd been content, or nearly so, with the snippy yet companionable interplay between her and Trey. In an odd way, she'd been his helpmate. They'd worked together to build something, a future of sorts rather than a fortune. The connection between them had been nebulous, but always there, hovering in the background. It seemed she'd found her place in life, a place where she belonged.

Gone, soon to be all gone.

"Now that we have that settled, shall we go rehearse this scene?" Derek surveyed her with calm satisfaction, as if he hadn't just destroyed her world. "It won't be difficult for you—I'll make sure of that. I find I get a better performance from the women I work with if they are happily involved with me."

Bettina had been right. Derek seemed to think he was a modern Svengali with every right to expect her submission to his will. It wasn't happening. She couldn't bear the thought, not after being close to Trey, making love in a meeting of hearts and minds—or at least her heart, her mind—instead of getting off in a meaningless joining of bodies.

"Not today," she said, meshing her fingers together before resting them on the table in front of her. "I would really like to hear more about these plans you have for me."

Let him think he'd won. If he figured she was resigned to being seduced by him and his promise of fame, what did it matter? It would give her time to decide what she was going to do about his threat.

One thing was for certain; she was not going to surrender without a fight, and she wasn't going to be his Zenobia.

There had to be a way out of this mess. All she had to do was find it.

CHAPTER THIRTEEN

*T*rey was a man on a mission. Striding into the exhibit building where the cantina for the movie people was located, he paused to allow his eyes to adjust to the dimness after the bright light outside. Zeni was supposed to be here somewhere, at least according to Gloria. He needed to find her. And if that interfered with Peabody's rehearsal plans for the morning, too bad.

He had just come from a confrontation with Granny Chauvin in the middle of Main Street. That elderly lady might stand no taller than the logo on his T-shirt, but she was formidable with her sharp eyes in their owl-like circles of wrinkles, her white hair flying around her head like feathers in the wind and her definite ideas about right and wrong.

She wasn't someone he wanted to tangle with when she

was annoyed.

"Tristan Thomas Benedict, what are you about with Zeni?" That demand was made the instant she spotted him. "I stopped in at the coffee shop yesterday, and there was that sweet girl with her ring finger as bare as a newborn baby's bottom. Explain yourself."

His cousin Beau had told him there would be days like this.

Granny had a way of interfering in everyone's love lives. She seemed to be good at it; if he remembered correctly, she'd had a hand in setting Beau and Carla on the right road.

"Yes, ma'am," he said. "It's just that—"

"I don't want to hear any excuses. You need to get that girl a ring before folks begin to think you've changed your mind. Or that she has, which is a lot more like it!"

Granny had a point, Trey was forced to admit. He should have thought about a ring. Thus his mission to find Zeni and make sure everything was the way it should be.

He could have chosen a ring himself and made a big production out of presenting it. However, that whole romance thing with the need to create unique memories didn't apply to their situation. He would feel ridiculous pretending that it did, and thought Zeni probably would as well.

No, he wanted Zeni to have something special, something that she'd really love and maybe keep for a long time. She seemed to have little jewelry other than costume pieces; he liked the thought of giving her something of value. That meant getting her input so the choice would be perfect.

There she was, at a table with Peabody. At least they were still in a public place, and it looked as if he'd caught her before the rehearsal could get started.

Zeni looked up and saw him weaving his way toward her through the tables. Relief and something more sprang into her face. An instant later, it was replaced by alarm.

Did he look that threatening? Trey didn't know, but he wasn't leaving without her.

"Zeni, honey," he said as he neared the table. "Something has come up. We need to go." The endearment was a small counterbalance to all the darlings and sweethearts used by Peabody, but gave him visceral satisfaction anyway.

"What is it? Is everything okay? Gloria hasn't burned down the Watering Hole?"

"Nothing like that. Just something we need to get done."

"Unless it's a matter of life or death," Peabody said with his trademark patronizing attitude, "Zeni is needed here."

Trey gave him a straight look. "Some things are more important than your movie. You might try remembering that next time you're tempted to interfere in people's lives."

The actor/director looked taken aback, but only for a second. "I must insist that Zeni honor her commitment to the project."

"And to you?"

"If you want to put it that way. We were about to have a private session to go over the part she'll be playing. She can't skip out of it on a whim."

Trey exchanged stare for stare with Peabody. "I think

she can. She's a free spirit and will stay that way." He turned his gaze to Zeni and held out his hand. "Ready?"

"I believe so," she said, and put her hand in his.

It was one of the greatest moments of his life when she tightened her grip and rose to stand beside him.

Peabody reached out and grabbed her other arm. "I don't think she really wants to go with you, or won't if she thinks about it."

Zeni was torn; that was plain to see. She was also gutsy. "Sorry, but you need to understand my position. Trey is the man I'm going to marry, after all."

Was there a reason he felt suddenly as if he was being used as a shield? It didn't matter. That was his purpose in all this, wasn't it?

"There you go," he said, holding Peabody's frustrated gaze.

"I demand that she stay here."

Trey leaned toward him and gripped his hand in a hard fist, flinging it away from Zeni's wrist. Keeping his voice low, he said, "I wouldn't do that if I were you. People might start to wonder what you're willing to do to make sure Zeni sees things your way, like maybe causing a convenient accident to eliminate the competition."

Peabody drew back. "I've no idea what you're talking about."

"Sure you do. It took place at the arena a few steps from where your motorhome is parked."

"If you're talking about that motorcycle crash, I can only suppose the man riding it didn't know what he was doing."

Trey could feel his blood pressure rising along with his temper. "That's your answer? Blame the man who was hurt?"

"I certainly had nothing to do with it!"

"But your people graded the arena the day before, and sent word it was ready for the trial run."

"That may be, but I refuse to allow you to make me responsible."

"I'll do better than that," Trey said leaning closer still. "I'll tell you to your face that the other bikers and I will be on our guard from now on. Nothing remotely like that so-called accident had better happen again. Here in Louisiana, plastic surgery is expensive for a face that's been rearranged."

Peabody was still sputtering his indignation when Trey walked away with Zeni keeping step beside him. They passed through the door and out into the mellow fall sunshine before he spoke again.

"I probably shouldn't have said that."

"You think?" Worry and doubt layered her voice.

"Or maybe I should. That's the point of the charade after all, isn't it? To rescue you from Peabody."

"I don't really know. It was your bright idea."

It was true she hadn't said she wanted rescuing, but he was doing it anyway. "And a good one it was, too. Seeing him back there, you'd think he was a hound dog deprived of a juicy bone."

The look she gave him was scathing. "I'm not anyone's bone."

"No, and I'd rather it stays that way."

They walked on a few steps before she gave him a side-long glance. "Would you really rearrange his face?"

"What do you think?"

"Too bad he didn't push it then," she said under her breath.

At least Trey thought that's what she said, though it didn't make good sense when she was still involved with the twice-damned movie. "What was that?"

She met his eyes, her own liquid with what might be distress. Her lips parted as if she was about to speak, then she closed them again and looked away. "Nothing. I just—I'm glad you showed up when you did."

So was he. That was, if she was glad. Still, he was fairly sure that wasn't what she'd been about to say.

He'd thought he was going to hear something important, and his heart began to throb like a ticking time bomb. That it came to nothing didn't slow it down by much.

He'd always known Zeni had her secrets. It was a disappointment that he wasn't about to discover one of them, but he'd get over it. He always did.

They reached the truck and he held the door for her. It was only after they left the fairgrounds parking lot and headed out of town that she spoke again.

"Where are we going?"

"To buy a ring," he answered, and made a story for her of the meeting with Granny Chauvin.

"I appreciate the thought, but I don't need a ring."

"It's not just for you. It's for Granny and everybody else,

so they'll believe it's serious."

"Including Derek, I suppose."

He shot her a stern look. "Especially for Peabody."

"And for you?"

"Me? No. What are you talking about?"

"For that traditional part of you that feels odd if you don't follow the rules, the part that needs to prove you're a man of your word to people like Granny Chauvin and the rest of Chamelot."

He might have been insulted if he hadn't understood her habit of misdirection so well, hadn't realized she was being snarky so he wouldn't think too much about whatever she'd decided not to tell him.

Never mind that there was a certain truth in her accusation.

"You can call it whatever you want," he said evenly. "But I'm still buying you a ring."

Pressing his lead foot down on the accelerator, he headed out of town.

CHAPTER FOURTEEN

*J*t appeared she was going to have an official token of their engagement whether she wanted one or not. Zeni wasn't sure why the idea disturbed her so much. It wouldn't make this fake engagement any more real.

Or maybe she did know. The whole thing was so false. To accept a ring she'd have to return in a matter of weeks made it worse.

If only she could bring herself to be honest with Trey, then all need for a ring would likely disappear. Problem solved.

If only.

She'd almost blurted out the cold hard facts, back there in the parking lot. What kept her from it she wasn't sure, unless it was the anger she'd sensed still simmering inside him. She couldn't stand the thought of having it directed at her.

It wasn't that she feared it; she'd made him angry dozens of times before. Yet being the center of his attention and protection for those few moments felt good, and she couldn't bear to see it change.

He'd threatened Derek. Watching the actor crawfish in the face of it had been amazing. It really had, even if she was fearful of what Derek might do to salvage his damaged pride.

Someday soon, maybe tomorrow or the day after, he'd throw what he had discovered about her in Trey's face and laugh about it.

She had more than one option to remove that possibility. Beyond revealing her past, she could tell Trey their fake engagement was off, that she was hell bent on being in Derek's movie. Then she could show up at the actor's motor home to rehearse for the part. Or for something, anyway.

It wouldn't be so bad, would it?

God, yes, it would.

But if she came clean with Trey, would it be any different? Leaving would be so much less painful than staying. What then? She could see how easy it might be to wind up in Derek's motor home on her way to L.A., anyway.

All right, but she couldn't just sit tight, do nothing and wait to see what happened.

Could she?

No. She had to decide what she was going to do, then get on with it.

In her preoccupation, it was some time before Zeni noticed they had left Chamelot behind. She was well aware there was a jewelry store in town. It was perfectly adequate for most gift occasions, and had a bridal area featuring china, crystal and silverware, as well as a decent selection of engagement rings. What did Trey have on his mind?

"Are we going to New Orleans?" Surprise was strong in her voice as she glanced at the houses and land that flashed past on either side of the road.

Trey met her eyes for an instant. "That a problem?"

"This is Gloria's full day, but I don't know how late she can stay."

"It's okay. She's got it."

"But if she needs to study—"

"She doesn't. It's all good, don't worry."

It seemed he had the situation under control; the coffee shop was in good hands. That should have been a relief. Instead, it made her question what else he had taken care of today. Had he changed the delivery date for the food supply order that was due this afternoon, or made payment arrangements for the guy who stocked the restrooms?

Had Trey made a reservation at one of New Orleans's many boutique hotels?

That possibility wasn't nearly as disturbing as it should be. A stolen afternoon, or maybe a whole night, with dinner at a nice restaurant followed by champagne, strawberries and chocolates from room service? Even if he was taking her for granted, she could think of worse endings for a high-handed shopping trip.

"No, it's no problem," she said at last.

The traffic was incredible once they reached the interstate, a steady barrage of kamikaze truck drivers, guys in Beamer's and Jags with Formula One aspirations, and women intent on serious shopping. To add to the problem, it began to rain, a steady downpour that cut visibility to less than 100 feet. Few of the drivers slowed for it. Trey decreased his speed somewhat, but still stayed in the flow.

Zeni might have been nervous with anyone else, but Trey was a good driver, his every move smooth and steady in spite of their speed. As the minutes passed, she was able to relax and even enjoy the patter of the rain on the truck's windshield and roof.

As she leaned against the headrest, admiring Trey's concentration on what he was doing, her gaze moved to his hands on the wheel. They were suntanned, long-fingered and capable, with a scar here and there; strong hands on a strong man. They had touched her, held her, given her such exquisite pleasure that she turned warm and moist just thinking about it.

She had never seen them caked with dirt or grease, though she knew he worked on his bikes and other vehicles, just as he intended to work on his grandfather's old house. Considering that was a lot more comfortable than her first thoughts.

"How many vehicles do you own?" The question was random, just something that wandered through her mind.

He sent her a surprised look. "What brought that on?"

"There's your dirt bike, the Harley, the small RV that's in

the garage and this truck," she plowed on without answering his question. "Is that all?"

"You left out the 1970 Plymouth Road Runner Super Bird, the muscle car I restored and set up to gain in value."

"Not exactly a family car. But then none of them are."

A thoughtful look crossed his face. "You're right. They're not."

She wasn't quite sure what he meant, whether it was a lack he meant to remedy or something he had no intention of ever correcting. She wasn't about to ask, as some things were better left alone. Turning her head, she gazed out at the rain soaked trees that sped past while trying not to think at all.

The downpour had passed over New Orleans by the time they reached the city. It was a good thing, as they had to park some distance away from the mall jewelry store Trey selected. Brightly lighted, with long rows of glass cases, it was typical of its kind.

The selection of engagement rings was vast, and the saleswoman helpful and knowledgeable, with a nice patter on cut, color and clarity. They were shown tray after velvet-lined tray of beautiful diamond engagement rings in an endless selection of shapes and cuts, from normal to the unusual, merely valuable to the outrageously priced.

They were all too glitteringly bright, too symbolic of every day engagements and weddings with their bridal gowns, bachelorette parties, bouquets and limousines; their hope and promise. They were also too expensive.

"Don't you see anything you like?" Trey asked when

Zeni had shaken her head at everything the salesperson presented.

"I like them all, but I just don't know."

"Then choose something to make a start, whatever grabs you at first sight."

"You choose, since this was your idea." She carefully avoided the saleswoman's raised-eyebrow curiosity.

"You're the one who will be wearing it."

"Yes, well, but they're all so—so bridal."

Trey gave her a harassed look. "So I should hope."

The saleswoman cleared her throat. With a carefully neutral expression, she said, "We have other selections that are less traditional. A lot of brides these days are choosing colored diamonds or gemstone and diamond mixtures."

Trey looked at her. Zeni shook her head. The saleswoman looked at both of them. They all stared down at the tray of diamond rings on the counter between them.

It was then that inspiration came to Zeni. With a glance at Trey from under her lashes she said, "I once knew a girl who found a beautiful ring at a pawn shop."

The saleswoman's sniff of disdain was perfectly audible. Trey ignored it, though he frowned while he held Zeni's steady gaze.

Abruptly his face cleared. "I have an idea."

He touched Zeni's arm, turning her toward the door, while thanking the saleswoman for her time. Moments later they were back in the truck and headed toward downtown New Orleans and the French Quarter.

Trey found a parking place in a small lot on Chartres

Street. As he opened the truck door for her, Zeni said, "What are we doing here? We passed two or three pawn shops."

"I know," he said, smiling down at her.

"The only one I remember in the Quarter used to be on Rampart Street, over on the Quarter's far side."

He shut the door behind her. "How long has it been since you were down here?"

"A while, really, but my mom and I rented an apartment in a small house on Dumaine until she died; she was a street artist, displayed her paintings on the railings of Jackson Square. I used to clatter up and down the streets of the Quarter by myself, knew nearly every shop owner and member of the police patrolman by their first names. I learned to cook by hanging around the back doors of restaurants."

"I didn't know that—you don't usually talk much about yourself."

No, she didn't, though it wasn't so much deliberate omission as a habit. She should change, starting now, since it was as good an opening as she was ever likely to find. She could save them both the time and effort of more ring shopping, and save Trey the money, too.

She met his eyes, clear gray and warm with something so much like affection that she felt her heart swell inside her. She scanned his face feature by feature, seeing the strength and dependability, and even a trace of nobility. Her gaze lingered on his lips, and her resolve wavered as she thought of the way he had kissed her, tasted her skin.

Words evaporated from her mind. She couldn't find the right ones, wasn't sure there were any.

"Are you hungry?"

He gazed down at her, waiting for an answer to that simple question. It was a moment before she could give it to him. There were, she knew, many kinds of hunger.

"Always," she said. "Always."

She had almost forgotten the rich layers of smells in the Quarter, the aromas of frying seafood and caramelizing sugar, old books, custom blended perfume and the scents of flowers from hidden gardens. She breathed it all in deep as she and Trey walked, while half-forgotten names, faces and happenings flitted through her mind.

There was the time she and her mother had danced in a sudden bath-water-warm summer shower that drenched them to the skin, and another when they bought shrimp the size of small lobsters fresh off the boat, boiled them with spices and lemons and dumped them in the sink to drain. The artsy clothes they couldn't afford, but bought anyway because they made them feel amazing. The Mardi Gras parade where Bacchus himself had thrown them whole handfuls of pearl necklaces. And more, so much more. The two of them had been unfettered and a little wild, until it suddenly ended. Though her mother was gone, Zeni was still all those things, she knew. Or she had been and would be again, if she could find the courage.

The wide-open French doors and thrown back shutters of a corner restaurant beckoned. They stepped inside where it was dim and cool, and the lazily turning ceiling fans stirred the aromas of frying onions, browning flour, chopped garlic and fresh-baked bread. They ordered typical French Quarter fare of gumbo and French bread served with chilled white wine, then topped it with bread pudding soaked in a buttery rum sauce.

Replete and strangely happy, they strolled on, winding up on Royal Street. Zeni noticed a pawn shop some distance ahead of them. That seemed most likely to be Trey's destination.

As they passed an antique shop, he glanced at the black and gold lettering on the window. "Let's look in here a minute," he said with an agreeably casual air. Without waiting for an answer, he stepped inside and held the door for her.

Zeni didn't mind. Anything worked for her as an excuse to delay choosing a ring. If it also gave her the chance to pretend a short while longer that she really was his fiancée, what was the harm?

The store seemed familiar. She realized after an instant that she had stood outside with her nose pressed against the glass when she was eleven or twelve. For a few moments of childhood yearning, she had gazed at all the treasures that once belonged to people who had extended families to know and love, and who had lived with and enjoyed all the beautiful and permanent furnishings for untold generations. Yet they were gone and their belongings discarded, becoming no more than the detritus of past lives.

Something of that same feeling remained inside her, though her thoughts went to the stored furnishings from

Trey's granddad's house. It must be comforting to live with those things when they held your family's memories. Yes, and when the memories themselves had special meaning, as they did to Trey.

Antique stores always had a certain smell, a combination of old wood, dust, furniture polish and countless hours, countless joys and tragedies. This one had something extra; the scent of the huge gray Persian that sat in the window. It seemed to belong in this Aladdin's cave of shimmering crystal chandeliers, polished mirrors, shining woods and gilded decorations.

A long glass counter with rosewood trim, a relic of some dry goods store from the distant past, sat to one side. A wizened lady of uncertain age stood behind it. She was elegant in black wool, cream silk and 18-karat gold jewelry. Her henna-tinted hair was knotted on top of her head and held by a gold pin, and she had a warm twinkle in her eyes.

"Welcome mademoiselle, monsieur, may I be of service?"

Zeni began to shake her head, but Trey jumped in ahead of her. "Do you have any Victorian era betrothal rings? Something in rubies and diamonds would be great."

"But of course as that was a favored combination. The hands of the ladies of that time were small, but that should not be a problem." The lady proprietor glanced at Zeni's slender fingers before she smiled and reached beneath her counter to pull out a tray of rings.

Zeni was distracted for a moment by the other vintage jewelry in the display case, marvelous cameos and bead necklaces of coral and jet; carved amethyst brooches and lockets set with seed pearls; watch chains with seals and mourning jewelry made of human hair. It was fascinating, far more so than the modern offerings available at the mall jewelry store.

"Zeni?"

She looked up to see Trey watching her, one hand on the display case beside the tray of rings and the other on his hip.

"Oh, sorry."

The lady behind the counter looked at Zeni again, and then studied the rings in front of her for a second. She picked up one and started to offer it, but Trey reached over and tapped a different one with slightly larger stones.

"Oh, yes, an excellent choice," she said, taking that one from its bed and holding it to the light. "The gold used is 18-karat, and the ruby is very fine, nicely clear, and the diamonds superior grade. Compared to similar modern versions, it's a truly great value at only—"

She stopped abruptly as Trey snapped a warning look in her direction. Continuing smoothly in her gentle, cultured tones, she covered the near gaffe by segueing into historical detail.

"Are you aware the Victorians considered the ruby as the gem of the heart? To their minds it stood for courage and love, particularly undying, passionate love. According to legend, rubies are hardened by fire, which gives them the power to kindle desire, you perceive."

Zeni looked up to meet the sympathy and understanding

in the woman's fine gaze. "Yes, I see," she murmured, almost to herself. She saw that the woman suspected a passionate relationship between her and Trey.

"A floral setting such as this one," the shop owner went on, "where the ruby is surrounded by diamonds like white petals around a red center, symbolized the heart of the home. That is to say, the wife who is always protected by the diamond-hard strength of the husband. It was all foolishness of course, but they were highly sentimental at the time." She paused. "I sometimes think they may have cared more for each other simply because there were fewer distractions—no TV, no video games, no internet or email—so they had more time to care."

Trey reached for the ring, and then took Zeni's hand in his. With a deft move, he slipped it onto her ring finger.

It felt so smooth and well-balanced. The fit was perfect, as if made for her. Zeni held it up to the light from the window and watched the shifting rich, burgundy-red gleams within the stone. It did look like a heart, one that was well and truly protected.

It was perfection in every way, and she was unbearably moved that Trey had chosen it for her, that he felt it was suitable for her. She would not be able to keep it, but she could wear it for a short while. There pain in the knowledge that it meant nothing, could never mean anything except a convenient arrangement. And yet she felt surrounded by a force-field of protection, something she could not have imagined and never explain.

Tears crowded her throat, pressing upward behind her

nose and into her eyes. She blinked but they would not go away.

Trey leaned to look into her face, his gaze searching. A faint smile curved his mouth and the gray of his eyes turned dark. Glancing up at the woman behind the counter he spoke in quiet satisfaction.

"We'll take it."

CHAPTER FIFTEEN

*T*rey was content. He had accomplished what he set out to do with this trip to New Orleans; he'd added an extra layer of protection for Zeni by buying her an engagement ring. He'd also found one he thought she might actually wear, which was a near miracle.

He'd been sure there for a while that he was going to come up short. Nothing had suited her. Nothing had really suited him, either. Yet both of them had fallen for the ruby and diamond ring.

It said something to him, though that might be because the woman in the shop had been a great sales lady. But it was mainly a perfect match for Zeni's personality; beautiful but just a little offbeat.

She had not taken it off since he put it on her finger. That was definitely in its favor and in his for coming up with the idea. Yeah, even if what she'd said about pawn shops had triggered it.

A pawn shop, for heaven's sake, as if he would be that cheap where she was concerned.

Okay, antique shops dealt in people's discards as well. There was a difference in his mind, however, between a ring traded in for money, and one that had likely been treasured as long as the wearer had a use for it.

He let his eyes rest on Zeni a moment where she walked beside him. Each time she looked down at the ring she smiled. For some reason that made him feel good inside.

To stay in the Quarter for the rest of the afternoon, have a nice dinner somewhere and then spend the night in a hotel, seemed like a fine idea. He'd love to extend their escape, to hold Zeni through the night—maybe see her wearing nothing except the ring.

He hesitated to mention it. The last thing he wanted was for Zeni to think he expected her to hop into his bed in return for his outlay today. Misplaced gratitude had no more purpose between them than misplaced obligation. He wanted her willing and eager or not at all.

"You about ready to head for home?" The question was as natural as he could make it while certain parts of his body objected, painfully, to every word.

"If you are."

"Not really, but I guess we're done."

"I should get back and relieve Gloria," she said in what had the sound of reluctant agreement.

That much was true. Gloria had been on duty since the early hours of the morning. To expect her to her close the place down for the night was too much.

"Then Midnight has been alone all day."

"The truck is this way then," he said, and crossed the street to head back toward Chartres.

Zeni was silent as they walked. He glanced at her once or twice, but she seemed to be watching the sidewalk in front of her in deep thought, rather than with her head up, taking in familiar surroundings as she had before. Was she disappointed that they were not staying? He'd like to think so, but it didn't quite feel right.

No, she had something on her mind, maybe the same thing she had almost mentioned earlier. He ran through every possibility he could think of, and there was only one she might not feel free to talk over with him. That one, he realized with grim recognition, was Derek Peabody.

It was possible she was upset with him for threatening the man. If so, it couldn't be helped; he wasn't about to apologize. On the other hand, there seemed no point in making things worse by bringing it out in the open.

"You okay?" he asked. "I'm not walking too fast for you?"

She looked straight ahead. "No I'm fine."

She wasn't. Trey knew that in part because of her low energy level, but also because she'd said nothing remotely annoying to him since they started out. There wasn't a lot he could do about it until she decided to open up about whatever was troubling her. She would eventually, he was sure; she had to if things were ever going to be right between them.

They didn't speak again until they reached the truck and

he helped her inside then moved around to the driver seat. He put the key in the ignition, but paused to look at her, his gaze moving over the shape of her there beside him, her face, before settling on the rich brown of her eyes. "You know I would never ask for more than you're ready to give, don't you, Zeni, never take advantage, never take anything for granted?"

"Yes, I know that." Her smile was warm and real, and yet so forlorn that it almost broke his heart.

"You will never guess what happened," Gloria said, her eyes shining like black glass. "I'm going to be in the dream scene with you in the movie!"

Zeni paused in the act of tying her apron strings, getting ready to take over the coffee shop from Gloria. "That's great, I'm really proud for you. But I thought you weren't interested."

"That was before I knew it was a paying gig," her waitress friend answered with a saucy grin.

"So how did it happen?"

"Derek Peabody himself came in while you were gone. He was looking for you—well, besides looking for lunch. Things were a little slow, and he started talking to me since you weren't available. He said something about how Mr. Trey had quit, wasn't going to be in it, and he needed another actor, someone who could dress things up a mite. He also said you'd mentioned how you might be able to find

198 | JENNIFER BLAKE

somebody for him. I figured, hey, why not me?"

"Good job," Zeni said in warm approval.

"You think it will be okay? I mean, who's going to mind the store, or at least cook and pass out food here and at the fairgrounds, if you and I are both busy with the movie?"

"Trey can probably handle it as long as I get up early to do the baking. But—you don't mind the role?" Zeni finished donning her apron and took onions from the bin to peel for the dinner setup.

"Lord, no. I can sit around and do nothing with the best of them. And they can call me anything they want as long as they give me a check afterward. I see a semester's tuition from this deal."

Zeni had to smile at that practical attitude. "I have to say, I'll be more than happy to have someone else around."

With any luck, the whole thing would be over in a day or two. Maybe then things could get back to normal.

Maybe she wouldn't have to have that talk with Trey, after all.

Maybe this whole engagement business would fade away.

Maybe she'd be happy about that, too. Eventually.

"I'll just bet you will," Gloria said on a laugh.

Zeni gave her a quick look, half afraid she had spoken out loud. "What do you mean?"

"I got this weird idea that the better I was at looking the other way around the movie set, the bigger my paycheck might be."

"You don't mean it?"

"Oh, but I do, girlfriend. Derek the Man has got some serious hots for you."

"He's just not used to being told no." Zeni stabbed the knife she held into a helpless onion and began to trim the root end so the pungent aroma rose around her. "And that's too bad, because the feeling is not mutual."

"Ain't that the way it goes?" Gloria wagged her head slowly back and forth. "You could maybe be a major player, half of one of those famous and fabulously wealthy Hollywood couples, except here you are lovesick for Mr. Trey."

"Gloria!"

"It's the truth isn't it? Though I can't for the life of me see a problem. You're nearly there, so make it all legal and church-like then go riding into the sunset on his Harley."

Zeni refused to look at Gloria while she put the big onion into the slicer and turned it into onion rings. "It isn't that easy."

"I don't see why not."

"It just isn't, okay? I'm not his kind, and never have been. I don't really belong and never will."

Gloria put a hand on one hip bone. "I don't think the boss man knows that."

"Doesn't matter, it's still the truth." Zeni went on at once in an attempt to change the subject. "So are you excited about the part? Do you have an appointment to see about a costume? And what did you think of Derek, now that you've talked to him up close and personal? Are you joining his fan club?"

"Who? Me? The man is seriously fond of himself, honey.

But yeah, I'm kind of excited. That snooty assistant of his is supposed to help me with a bed sheet or some such thing to use as a costume. But I seriously think you need to get yourself one of those chastity belts to wear while you do this scene with our Derek. No telling what he might try. Not much I'd put past him, not much at all."

Zeni hardly knew whether she wanted to laugh or cry, though she realized a second later it was the onion that was causing the tears. With a watery chuckle, she reached for a paper towel to dry her eyes.

Gloria screamed, a high-pitched sound of amazement, and reached to grab Zeni's hand. She turned the ring she wore to the florescent light above the sink. "You sly little devil you! Is this what I think it is?"

"Depends on what you think it is." Zeni wriggled her fingers, trying to release them.

"Looks like an engagement ring to me. Don't tell me it's just a birthday present or something."

Zeni glanced at the ruby and diamonds shining on her hand, and couldn't help smiling. "It could be, couldn't it?"

"Nope. No way. Looks too much like something Mr. Trey would buy for you. I am *that* relieved, since I thought the two of you were a tad casual about the whole thing the other day. So when is the wedding, and do I get to be a bridesmaid—and maybe plan a knockout bachelorette party?" Dropping Zeni's hand, she began to do a fast happy dance in the middle of the kitchen.

"Don't get too excited," Zeni said after a second of watching in amusement. "It's just a different version of that chastity belt you mentioned."

Gloria stopped. "What are you saying? Mr. Trey asked you to marry him right here where we're standing. I heard him with my own ears."

She'd said too much. It was unintentional, but couldn't be helped. Besides, Gloria was too good a friend and coworker, too close to both her and Trey not to know the truth. Zeni told her as simply as possible. "So you see," she ended, "the ring is real enough. It just doesn't mean anything."

"Aw, now, I'm totally bummed. It's too damned bad—so bad I'd like to smack Derek myself. But I still think Mr. Trey likes you a lot."

"I like him too," Zeni said quietly.

Gloria put both hands on her hips this time. "Well then?"

"Well, nothing. And I think I need to take better care of this ring." Removing the priceless antique, she slid it into her pocket while summoning a smile. "Onion juice and tears probably aren't doing it any good. Or me, either, if it comes to that."

That conversation with Gloria came back to Zeni often over the next couple of days. It would be beyond wonderful if she could believe Gloria was right, and Trey felt something for her.

She couldn't quite accept it. In her world to date, things had never been quite that easy.

A single rehearsal was called for the dream sequence. It took place while Derek was in Los Angeles at some meeting of the movie's backers. The relief of that was stupendous, even if his assistant, Bettina, was more critical of her and Gloria's performances than the actor might've been. She was also more forthcoming about camera angles, bits of business, and particularly the filming schedule for this scene, which she said would begin on the day after the ring tournament.

The last was good news. The end seemed to be in sight. It appeared to Zeni that she might actually reach it unscathed. She wasn't quite sure why Derek had made himself so scarce, though she had to wonder if the plastic surgery threat had as much to do with it as his business interests.

Plans for the medieval fair proceeded without letup. Several committee meetings were held at the Watering Hole, some calm and some not, as ways and means of working around the needs of the movie company were decided. A faery queen was chosen, along with her ladies. Booths were knocked together, decorated and set up out at the fairgrounds. Crafts and baked goods with English names, if no English origins, were stockpiled. Everyone who owned a sewing machine overheated it as they sewed yard upon yard of velvet, silk and satin polyester or fake leather for costumes.

The fair weekend finally arrived, kicked off by the annual parade. Its various floats rolled down Main Street in all their splendor and tackiness, a cavalcade led by a police escort, fire trucks with blasting horns, and several cars of waving, candy throwing politicians.

The whole thing was more splendid than in past years, and had better participation because it included a float representing the movie. This was a glorious thing decked out with real flowers, giant replicas of burning candles, and a huge image of Shakespeare in recognition of the film's title, *Brief Candles,* even if any connection to the Bard's work was purely accidental.

The parade route was also noisier, since Trey's bicycle club put in an appearance, riding in a group on their Harleys to remind folks about the ring tournament. It was a cool day, one of the first of the fall season, and the guys wore new black motorcycle jackets, each embroidered with a shield superimposed upon an outline of the state of Louisiana and the name they had recently given themselves, the Louisiana Knights.

Zeni was supposed to be on duty, though the coffee shop was empty. She ran for her camera as the motorcycle club roared down the street, circling, stopping and starting, popping the occasional wheelie as they kept to the parade's slow pace. On the sidewalk outside, she ran into Carla and Mandy, both with their cameras clicking as they immortalized the floats while waiting for Beau and Lance to come even with where they stood.

"They look incredible, don't they?" Carla said with a fond smile. "The ring tournament tonight should be something."

That was the expectation, one that had caused it to be set as the opening event for the fair. That it wasn't exactly medieval was also a factor. The committee wanted it out of the way so it wouldn't steal attention from the more authentic tumbling, jousting and mock melee that would follow.

The high expectations made Trey nervous, however, as Zeni well knew. He was afraid the tournament might not be as sensational as some envisioned, so people would be disappointed.

"Love the jackets. When did they have them made?" Zeni stepped out onto the brick cobbled street for a long-distance shot as she spoke.

"They were delivered by the little brown truck last night," Mandy said, her attention on the photo screen of her phone.

"Jake came up with the idea, and even drew the logo," Carla added. "Too bad Beau is getting to wear their cousin's jacket before he does."

Zeni lowered her phone to meet Carla's compassionate gaze. "I was going to ask about Jake. He's still doing okay, right?"

"Good enough, though he's had a few short and not-so-sweet words to say about the neck brace he's being forced to wear. Fair committee wanted him to ride on the movie company float and throw candy to the kids, but his doctor advised against it. He's in the lead police car with Lance's chief deputy."

"That's his Harley that Beau's riding then?"

"It is," Carla said in dry agreement, "though he gave it a thorough going over to be sure it was no worse for the accident. Beau will be taking his place in the tournament, too."

"Really?"

Mandy entered the conversation then. "And of course Lance, not to be outdone, will also be competing."

"That's mainly to support Trey. One of the other guys dropped out, claiming it was too dangerous. Lance is taking that man's place."

"If you say so." Mandy pulled a face at Carla. "I still think he just couldn't stand being left out of the excitement."

"Or to pass up such a great excuse for being on hand in case something goes wrong?"

"There is that."

Zeni, listening to the two of them, recognized the worry behind their dry comments. The thought of another accident made her feel cold inside. "Lance really thinks something might happen?"

Mandy looked grim. "He doesn't know, but he's taking no chances. Extra security has been added."

"You don't mess with a Benedict in Tunica Parish," Carla said with a nod.

All that should've been reassuring, but wasn't. If the first so-called accident had been directed at Trey, then why wouldn't whoever was behind it try again?

"Speaking of the tournament, you'll be there, won't you?" The question came from Mandy, but Carla also turned her head to look at Zeni in lively expectation.

"Oh, yeah. No way I'd miss it."

"Then you should come and sit with us since all the guys will be on the field. We Benedict women have to stick together."

Benedict women.

Trey Benedict's woman.

Zeni's throat closed up tight at the idea of it. She didn't deserve the title or belong to that elite group, but could pretend for now. Too soon, the day would come when pretending would be at an end.

"That—that will be great," she said finally. "Absolutely perfect."

CHAPTER SIXTEEN

*T*he weather gods smiled on Chamelot for the beginning of the fair; not only had it been warm and sunny with low humidity during the parade, but the night was just as pleasant for the ring tournament. Not too cool and not too warm, it came with a nice breeze that cleared the air of gnats and mosquitoes. The wind also stirred the brightly colored pennants on poles that were set up around the arena and was natural air conditioning for the people that crowded onto the open bleachers of weathered gray wood.

Attendees kept pouring in, filling the walkways, lining the open space behind the highest benches and using the steps as seats. Beyond the tournament itself, the fact that the event was going to be filmed was a major attraction. Folks gazed around at the two huge cameras set up at each end of the announcement booth and others filling strategic spots, and figured out that amount of camera power meant a person could be caught on film at any minute. They could all turn out to be extras in *Brief Candles*, now couldn't they?

The town baseball field had been robbed of its stadium lights to supplement those on four sides of the arena. The school's band, heavy on the brass, was set up below the announcement booth. That booth, with its commanding view, had been taken over by the movie crew. Derek, back from California, was plainly to be seen in the bank of lights along the front. His assistant, also on hand, moved around him like a satellite caught in his magnetic orbit.

As Zeni emerged from the entranceway between the bleachers, she waved at Gloria who was sitting with some of her friends, also at Granny Chauvin with one of her grandsons. A shout from above drew her attention then. It was Mandy, waving with both arms to catch her attention, and pointing at the seat between her and Carla.

The location the two Benedict wives had secured was super, the equivalent of sitting at the 50-yard line if this were a football game. Three rows up from the railing that kept people from falling into the arena, it allowed a good view over the heads of the standees gathered there.

"How did you get such good seats? You must've been here since the middle of the afternoon." Zeni's greeting for Mandy was admiring and a little breathless from pushing through the crowd and climbing bleachers.

"Almost," Lance's wife agreed with a grin. "Carla and I took turns holding the seats. It's great that you made it. We had about decided we'd missed seeing you come in."

"I'd have been here sooner, but I had to chase customers out of the Watering Hole before I could close the doors."

"That's the way it goes," Carla said in wry understanding.

What Zeni failed to mention was that she'd also waited to see if Trey meant to come by before going to the fairgrounds, maybe to eat a little something first. He hadn't showed. It was silly to be disappointed when she suspected he was checking the arena one last time, but she was anyway.

"You made it before the guys come riding in and things get started, which is what matters," Mandy said, and reached out to touch her hand as Zeni sat down beside her.

It was good of her to try to make her feel better, but that was Mandy. She liked it when everyone was included, as with her invitation this morning. Looking at her and Carla now, however, Zeni didn't feel much like she belonged. She had come as she was in her denim skirt and tank top. By contrast, Carla appeared cool and sophisticated in cream colored pants and a pale blue silk shirt and Mandy wore a loosely fitted dress in pink linen. They were all southern style and charm and she was—what? Not exactly trailer trash, though not far from it.

"Listen," Carla said, cocking her head to one side. "I think that's the guys now."

Faint above the noise of the crowd could be heard the steady drone of engines. The sound grew louder and more commanding. Hearing it, people in the bleachers quieted and craned their necks, trying to discover the source. The rumbling became a roar that seemed to shake the stadium lights on their stands and echo like thunder against the dark night sky above.

The shrill sound of a whistle cut through the noise. Abruptly, the band struck up a spirited rendition of "Born to Be Wild."

Zeni looked toward the bandstand with everyone else. That was, until she noticed that the movie cameras were focused on a white gate directly across from where she and the other women sat. She turned in time to see that barrier slide open, and to glimpse movement and vibrating lights in the darkness beyond it.

In they came, riding in single file, nine men on custom-painted Harleys, strong and erect yet at ease on their powerful machines. They circled the arena once, twice, and a third time. Then they swung to a halt, one by one, and lined up in a row in front of their gated entrance, each machine a precise distance from the other, each man balancing with his legs at the same angle. In unison, they removed their matching helmets with black gloved hands and held them in the crooks of their left arms.

Gone were the leather jackets of the morning. In their place, the riders wore long-sleeved black shirts covered by tunics of silver chain mail, and black leather pants with black boots. From the shoulders of the tunics hung short cloaks of black edged in metallic silver lamé and centered by the map and shield logo of the Louisiana Knights.

They were impressive and dramatic; Zeni knew she should've been proud. She was, and yet she had to choke down the stupid rise of tears.

Applause broke out, a tumultuous welcome and gesture of warm, hometown appreciation for the display. As it went on and on, Zeni leaned toward Mandy, speaking under its cover. "I thought they were supposed to be wearing metal armor and old-style knight's helms."

"They were, but our guys got their heads together and decided the armor was too bulky and the helms made it hard to see. They put the problem to Peabody's people, and they came up with the chain mail and normal helmets instead."

"Because of Jake's accident, too, I suppose."

"In part, though he'd have been fine except for that board covered by dirt. Mainly it was for better safety all around."

She should've known about the change, might have if she'd seen more of Trey since the New Orleans trip. He'd been in and out at the coffee shop but was always in a hurry, always had some of the bikers with him. She'd wondered if he was regretting their weird engagement or maybe the expensive ring he'd bought, but hadn't wanted to ask. It seemed needy for one thing, but he also owed her nothing. More than that, the odd situation between them would soon be over. If they weren't too lovey-dovey when together, as in recent days, it might not come as a huge surprise when the engagement came to nothing.

And if she missed him with a deep, persistent ache, no one needed to know it, least of all Trey.

The sound system squealed as a microphone

malfunctioned. It was a signal that the mayor was about to speak. Standing in the booth's glare of lights, she raised her hands for quiet and waited for the band to come to a stopping place. She welcomed everyone to the tournament and to the opening of the medieval fair. With the most profound pleasure, she introduced the knights who would be riding in the modernized version of the ring tournament.

They appeared as knights indeed as their names were called out one by one, standing so tall and somehow noble astride their motorized steeds while the night wind lifted their hair and waved the cloaks that hung from their wide shoulders. They were everything that was inventive and hardworking, daring and courageous.

And there was Trey in the center of the line, with Beau on one side and Lance on the other. Trey, who had given her a job, a place to live and his friendship when she had no one, and who had done nothing except protect her while asking nothing in return. Trey, the truest knight of them all, at least in her eyes.

Zeni's heart swelled inside her as she watched him, throbbing in painful bursts with the knowledge that she loved him and had for a long time. She loved him, no matter how she'd denied it or had fought against it. She loved him, for what good it did her, or ever would.

Now the mayor was introducing a young high school girl who would sing the national anthem. She did a far better job of it with her sweet, clear voice and simple phrasing than many a recording star tapped for some major event. The invocation was given by a local pastor. Finally, her honor the mayor welcomed the producer/director and star of the marvelous upcoming movie *Brief Candles* to Chamelot yet again, told him how delighted the town was to be chosen for his film, and turned the floor over to him for an explanation of exactly what a ring tournament was and how it fit into the movie he was filming.

Derek actually did a fair job of it, not too surprising since he was a showman of sorts with an actor's trained voice. It helped, no doubt, that he had his speech written out in front of him.

The ring tournament had a long history in Louisiana, he said, one dating from the Romantic Period of the nineteenth century until at least two decades after the Civil War. Tonight's tournament with Harleys instead of horses was a definite departure from tradition, but would follow the same general rules as in the old days. Each biker would be given a lance. One after the other, the riders would then use them to spear the rings that were suspended from a large arch located in the center of the field. As each ring was taken, it would remain on the rider's lance. The riders would continue until all rings were collected. There would be three different rounds of nine rings each, and the arch holding the rings would be changed between each round. The rider who had the most rings collected on his lance at the end of the final round would be declared the winner of the tournament and given the opportunity to crown his ladylove queen of the tournament.

Derek paused for applause from the crowd at this development, but went on again. The ring tournament was being

214 | JENNIFER BLAKE

filmed for *Brief Candles* as one of several dream sequences in the script, he said. It might not be used in its entirety, but would serve a vital and colorful purpose. His production company appreciated the opportunity to work in this fine community, and was grateful to the Louisiana Knights for allowing him to film their tournament. He and his entire staff saluted their skill and daring. He was sure it was a spectacle that would be long remembered in Chamelot and wherever the film might be shown. He wished them all the best of luck, and would leave them with that ancient challenge: May the best man win!

It happened more or less as described.

The riders rode to the far side of the arena, on Zeni's right. The great arch was moved into position, one made of what appeared to be PVC pipe that had been spray-painted silver and set on wheels. From its center hung nine evenly spaced silver rings hanging on heavy cords, shining in the lights.

The rings weren't that large, being about the diameter of one of Zeni's big hoop earrings. She thought that's exactly what they might be for a moment, but Carla said they were actually heavier. They had come from the plumbing shop where Beau bought his greenhouse supplies and, like the arch, spray-painted silver for effect.

The riders lined up in single file. The first man was given a lance, perhaps ten feet long, tapered from the point to the hilt and decorated in colors that matched his bike. As he took off, carrying it while he circled the arena once, twice, and a third time to gather speed before racing toward the rings, the next man in line received his lance. So it went, one man after the other, circling, circling in ever increasing noise and dust, ever increasing smells of churned sand and engine fumes. After a few minutes it was almost impossible to tell the men apart; they looked so similar with their same costumes, same helmets, same speeding bikes—though a few machines had colored LED lights that gave some hint of identity when they could be seen through the dust.

The audience got into it. A correctly caught ring was greeted with shouts, whistles and applause, while a miss that set the ring swinging earned groans of sympathy and calls of better luck next time. People tried to keep count, but the rings slid down to lodge halfway to the hilt, making them difficult to see, difficult to track given the constant movement of the bikes. Added to that, the mobile cameramen often blocked the view. Irate audience members began to yell at them to get out of the way, to go home, go back to Hollywood. Before they knew it, however, all the rings had been collected and the first round was over.

Vendors came out while the arch was wheeled away to be reloaded with rings for the second round. Moving among the crowd, they sold fall favorites of candied apples, popcorn balls rich with molasses and butter, bags of roasted peanuts and cotton candy. Cold drinks were provided to wash it all down, but no beer; it was a family outing after all. Everyone was exhorted to eat, drink and be merry, because the proceeds would be used to defray the expense of extra security for the fair and the movie company. Most paid attention, since the delectable smells wafting over the crowd were enough to make anyone hungry. Anyone, that is, except Zeni; apprehension tied her stomach in such knots that she couldn't even think about it.

The bikers had removed their helmets to take a water break. It was a necessity, no doubt, because of the dust that formed a golden haze in the lights, stirred up by the spinning wheels.

Zeni sought and found Trey with her gaze. He was watching her, she saw, and lifted her hand to give him a quick wave. Smiling, he tipped the neck of his water bottle in her direction in a small salute.

She couldn't look away. It was a small thing, that proof that he had thought of her in the midst of the tournament, that he knew she was there, knew where she was seated. Yet her chest ached with the bright pleasure of the moment, and she knew it was one she would always remember.

The second round was basically a replay of the first. Though the crowd cheered the successes, their main concern now was with who was winning. They seemed to miss the scoreboard provided by most sports, and the ring count updates, announced by the mayor, were so slow in coming they were obsolete by the time they were given. That was, when they could be heard above the constant engine noise.

A fair-sized contingent seemed restless, as if they'd half expected something more from the event, maybe a confrontation between the bikers, a major spill, or even a disaster such as the accident at practice that injured Jake. Some few left, especially those who could not find seats, filing down and out from behind the highest bleachers.

During the intermission before the final round, the band entertained with the raucous tune, "Get Your Motor Running." As the event headed toward its end and Zeni's nervous stomach began to settle, she succumbed to temptation and bought a popcorn ball. She nibbled at it while watching Trey check his bike along with those of his cousins and friends, still guarding against mishap. It looked as if they were almost home free on that front, however, and she was able to enjoy her sweet and salty confection with a lighter heart.

Around and around the bikes went for Round Three. Zeni managed to keep her eyes on Trey this time, though they burned with the effort. He was racking up the rings in fine style, yet so were Lance and Beau. The final score was going to be close.

At last it was over. The last ring was snatched onto a lance; all the rings of this third round had been collected, leaving their empty cords dangling from the arch. The mayor and members of the medieval fair committee descended to the arena floor for the official count from each biker's lance.

While that was going on, Zeni glanced up at the announcer's booth, wondering if that part was being filmed. If so, a lot of footage would require editing. As far she could tell, the cameras were still rolling; she could see the cameramen behind them. Derek and Bettina must've grown bored and left, however, as they were nowhere in sight.

Finally, the count was done. The mayor mounted to the booth again to announce the winner. Against all expectation, it was a three-way tie between Beau, Lance and Trey, each having the maximum number of rings that could be collected. But in the generous spirit of true knights, so the mayor declared, two of the winners relinquished their claim to the honor of crowning the queen of the tournament. They insisted the prize should go, uncontested, to the man who had originated the idea of the ring tournament. That man was Chamelot's own Trey Benedict.

The band director apparently had a sense of humor. The instant the mayor ceased to speak, he picked up his baton and led the members in a thunderous yet melodious version of "The Horse." With that as their theme, Lance and Beau, led by Trey, began their victory laps, roaring around the arena three abreast, once, twice, and then a third time.

But then Lance and Beau peeled away, leaving Trey to ride alone to the riotous applause of the crowd. The noise grew deafening as he finished his victory lap and swerved to send his bike wheeling toward where Zeni sat.

Mandy and Carla, their faces alight with good humor, urged her to her feet and down to the railing just above the dirt floor. At the same time, Trey halted his bike, cut the engine and set the kickstand. Stripping off his gloves, he pulled a gold circlet from inside his tunic and displayed it to the crowd for an instant.

It flashed in the stadium lights, a modest and simple yet elegant tiara, not at all tacky. Zeni stared at it, euphoria and dread fighting it out inside her. It was true that most people in town knew she and Trey were engaged, but it was still a semi-private arrangement. Giving her this crown, claiming her in public as his ladylove, was an acknowledgment from Trey on a par with putting an announcement in the local paper and sending out wedding invitations; it would make it twice as difficult to end what was between them. Yet it was such a precious and moving prospect that she would not have changed it even if she could.

Trey walked forward with the crown in his hands and warm anticipation in the deep gray of his eyes. The band muted the last strains of its theme. The jubilant celebration of the crowd began to fade as they waited to hear what he might say, but also to see what Zeni would do.

It was then the popping noise came, like firecrackers going off. She heard a buzzing over her head. Sand kicked up around Trey. He started forward, his face grim as he stared up at the bleachers above her.

"Down, Zeni," he shouted, "Get down!"

A final explosion sounded then. Trey stopped as if he'd hit a wall. He clamped a hand to his chest, clenching a fistful of the chain mail that draped it. He staggered, spun in slow motion. He crashed full length on the sand of the arena.

The crown he held flew from his hand, rolling in a dazzle of light. It struck the foot of the railed bleachers. It settled there, half-buried in the dirt, six feet below Zeni.

It was, like Trey, far beyond her reach.

CHAPTER SEVENTEEN

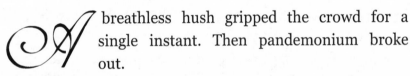

A breathless hush gripped the crowd for a single instant. Then pandemonium broke out.

Screams, yells and the crying of children rose above the dull roar of exclamations and questions without answers. The mayor seized the microphone to call for calm, but the plea was ignored. People surged to their feet, pushing and shoving, stampeding toward the exit. They had expected excitement, but not like this. Too many crazy shootings by demented gunmen had been in the news in the past months.

Zeni moved with the maddened rush until she reached the short flight of steps down to the ground. Just beyond was the gateway into the arena. She fought her way to it, but it was padlocked. Without hesitation, she climbed over and dropped to the sand on the other side.

Her mind was clear; she had no time for panic or terror, no time for useless speculation. She had to get to Trey; that was all that mattered. Thinking or feeling could wait until she knew there was nothing she could do for him, nothing to be done by anyone.

From ground level, the open space of the arena with its windswept sand and glaring lights seemed vast, much bigger than from the bleachers above. The knot of people where Trey had fallen looked far away. She ran toward them, but seemed to make little progress, as if the air had congealed, holding her back. She could make out Trey's long form sprawled on the ground, overshadowed by his friends; could see Beau kneeling beside him; Beau who was an EMT with the emergency squad and the local hospital. A sob caught in her throat as she saw that his hands gleamed red with blood.

Behind her, calling after her, others were running, running, as she was. Carla and Mandy she thought, in a distant part of her mind; Gloria, too, and the deputies who had been on duty at the entrance, even Granny Chauvin somewhere to the rear. She couldn't stop, couldn't wait for them.

Abruptly, she was where she wanted to be. A final lunge, and she fell to her knees next to Trey. She picked up his hand and eased closer, holding it as she blinked back tears.

He was so still, so white under his tan, all the power and vital force of his personality vanquished. His fingers were cold and lax in hers, without any sign of strength or movement. Blood shone wetly against the black of his shirt in the floodlights, beneath the red-stained chain mail he still wore, perhaps to keep from moving him. His wound was covered by a thickly folded pad Beau pressed to his chest, one made of the cloak he'd worn for the tournament.

Zeni glanced at Trey's cousin. Horror leaped inside her as she saw the sympathy in his face. Her voice strangled in her throat, she asked, "Is he—?"

"No. He's breathing, but going into shock."

"Has someone called—?"

Thankfully, he didn't allow her to finish that thought, either. "An ambulance is on its way. Lance is outside, clearing the parking lot so it can get closer."

It shouldn't take long to arrive. The hospital wasn't that far away. Nothing was any great distance in Chamelot.

"I thought—that was shots I heard, wasn't it?"

"Yeah, he was shot."

She clasped Trey's hand closer, rubbing her palm over the backs of his fingers as if she could lend him some of her warmth. Staring down at his features that she knew so well, the broad brow, the straight nose, the sensual mouth, she tried to memorize them, though they kept blurring. Tears splashed down onto their joined hands. She barely noticed the others around her, standing over her, until a quiet question from Mandy snagged her attention.

"Did anyone see where the shots came from? I mean, most of you down here on the arena floor were facing in that direction."

The other riders shook their heads, muttering negatives with the sound of regret and self-blame. They had been watching Trey and what he was about to do, they said.

They'd thought any danger, any chance of anything |happening, was over.

Zeni looked up. "They came from up higher in the bleachers, I think, maybe behind the last row. I'm not exactly sure, but somewhere like that." She paused, then went on in semi-coherence. "I didn't see the person, but I—I know it's crazy, but I noticed something while the rings were being counted."

"What?" Beau demanded in quiet authority when she came to a halt.

She bit her bottom lip, uncertain that what she'd seen had anything to do with Trey lying there with a bloody wound in his chest. But then she went on anyway.

"Derek Peabody wasn't—no one was in the booth except the cameramen."

Beau, still exerting pressure on Trey's chest, turned his head to say something over his shoulder. Immediately, four or five of the bikers whirled away, heading toward the stands where Zeni had been sitting and where the bleachers were now almost empty. It seemed unlikely the shooter was still around, unless it was to gloat over his handiwork, but they might gain some idea of where he'd stood, where he'd set up for his target, and how he'd gotten there.

Zeni had no time to think about it. The wail of an ambulance could be heard, growing steadily louder. Within seconds, uniformed ambulance personnel hustled in from the back entrance, rolling a stretcher toward them with dust kicking up from every wheel.

She wasn't allowed to go with Trey in the ambulance.

She wanted to insist, but knew it was better if she didn't risk being in the way if intervention was needed. The emergency was dire enough already.

She rode with Mandy instead, following Lance in his patrol SUV with its lights flashing and siren blasting out to clear the way ahead. The drive was almost as fast as the ambulance, as the sheriff spearheaded a phalanx of bikers, friends and neighbors in that high-speed dash through town. In mere minutes, he was also leading a mass invasion of the emergency room.

They were in time to catch up with the ambulance crew as they wheeled Trey straight back toward the trauma room. They stopped long enough for Zeni to touch his face, drop a brief kiss on his forehead, and whisper in his ear. Then he was taken away, rolled at warp speed beyond the double doors that allowed no admittance.

They waited, Lance and Beau, Mandy and Carla, Gloria and Granny Chauvin and a dozen more. They sent or answered text messages, and stepped outside to receive or make cell calls. They poured coffee and let it get cold; picked up magazines, flipped through them, and put them down again. Some prayed, silently or aloud.

Beau, being a privileged figure around the hospital, went to ask for a report now and then, and came back each time with no news other than that Trey was holding his own. Lance was in and out, cycling between his office's crime scene investigation and the hospital. With Beau and one or two others, he speculated on who, how and why, and went over and over the run-in between Derek and Trey about

Jake's accident. Jake himself, on hearing the news, had himself driven from Turn-Coupe to join them with his neck in his padded brace, anxious to learn all they could tell him.

Basically, everyone paced, talked, and sometimes laughed aloud from sheer nerves. A few had to leave as the first hour, and then another, passed. Others took their places. But mostly, they all waited.

Zeni knew everyone who was there. Though she sat and stared at nothing, said little, she felt their caring and concern and was grateful to be with them, a part of a loving community that was like family in all the ways that mattered. She was one of them for these long minutes and hours, at least, and she was glad, so very glad to be within their tight circle.

At last the surgeon came out, still in his green scrubs and with protective bootees covering his shoes. He seemed at a loss as to where to direct his report. That was until Granny Chauvin, sitting next to Zeni and holding her hand, spoke up.

"This is Zeni over here, doctor, Trey's future bride. She's the one who most needs to hear what you got to say."

It wasn't true; everyone there had as much or more right than she did. With a quick glance around, she said, "I think we all need to know, if you don't mind."

The surgeon nodded, his face sober. "Trey came through the surgery okay, and is in recovery. He has two broken ribs and a bruised spleen, plus a large abrasion, actually a long gouge, caused by the bullet as it hit the chain mail he was wearing. That steel mesh might not have deflected a direct hit, but it probably saved his life since the round was traveling at an angle."

"What kind of round?" Lance asked, his voice grim.

"Lightweight rifle, it looks to me, most likely a .22." He dug into the pocket of his scrubs and pulled out a misshapen slug that he passed over to Lance. "Doesn't help a lot, I know, but there it is. Rifles like that will likely show up in half the closets in town, leftover from when men were teens. Trey's lucky it was nothing larger."

"Yeah," Lance said. "It's also a good thing the shooter was either nervous or a bad shot, since it took four rounds at least to find the range."

Zeni put a hand to her mouth, feeling warm tears slide down her face to pool against its edge. Close, it had been so close. It was a moment before she could control her voice enough to form words. "He—he's really going to be all right?"

"Trey's strong and comes from good, healthy stock." The doctor nodded in the direction of the cousins. "I'd say he'll be up and around in a couple of days, and back to his old self before the month is out. That's as long as he stays away from motorcycle sports."

CHAPTER EIGHTEEN

*T*rey knew where he was the instant he opened his eyes. The unmistakable smells of antiseptic wipes, cleaning compounds and human misery penetrated the darkness of his unconsciousness long before he opened his eyes and was "at himself," as his granddad used to say. It was no surprise to see the dangling lines of fluids attached to him here and there, or the blinking lights of monitors.

What was unusual was the faint but persistent whiff of perfume that almost neutralized the hospital odors. That fragrance had been the stuff of his dreams for months; he would recognize it anywhere.

Turning his head on his pillow, he found the source. Zeni was sitting in a chair pulled up beside his bed. She'd leaned to rest her folded arms on the mattress, and was asleep with her head pillowed upon them. It was no wonder; night blackness peeped through the louvers of the window blinds behind her, along with the distant sheen of a streetlamp. His internal clock told him it was after three in the morning or perhaps a little later. She had a right to be tired.

It took more effort than he expected to lift and move his hand. Still, he managed it, was able to touch the silky brown hair that spilled across his sheets. He gathered the warm strands in his hand, holding them like a lifeline as his eyelids slowly closed again.

The next time he woke the room was bright with daylight, the blinds were open and a clattering breakfast cart was being pushed through the door. The nurse in scrubs behind it was short, pleasantly rounded and had nice eyes, but was entirely too cheerful. The main problem with her was she was not Zeni.

Trey frowned at her, his mood more than a little grouchy. "Where is—"

"Oh good," Zeni exclaimed as she emerged from the bathroom that opened next to the entrance of his private room. "I was hoping coffee would get here before he woke up."

"I'm awake," he said as a reminder that no one needed to talk over him.

"So you are, and about time," the nurse said with a smile. "You've no idea how glad we all are to see it."

How could he stay cantankerous or uncooperative in the face of that attitude?

Trey lay supine, allowing his hands to be washed for

him, his head to be raised, and the breakfast tray to be rolled across his lap. He was quiet while Zeni removed the plastic wrap from what appeared to be oatmeal, opened his carton of milk and put a little butter on his toast. He drew the line at having his coffee cup held for him or being fed, but was a model patient otherwise.

He had to be, because it was the best way to get rid of the nurse so he could talk to Zeni. The instant her pleasingly plump figure disappeared through the door, he demanded to know exactly what had happened.

She told him without mincing too many words, which was exactly the way he wanted it. He wasn't hungry, though he sipped his coffee and pretended to eat while she talked. The nagging ache that started up in his chest when he woke the second time had become a raging pain, but he ignored it. The last thing he wanted was some high-powered, fast-acting painkiller to dull his senses, maybe even put him under again.

"You're not eating," she said, pausing in the middle of telling him how his cousins and half the people he knew had waited until all hours to find out whether he was going to live or die.

He took a bite of toast. "Yes I am."

She reached to put a finger under his chin to bring his head up so he was forced to meet her eyes. "You're hurting. You need something for pain."

He didn't know how she could be so sure, but he wasn't having it. "Not yet. So all these folks went home and left you here to sit with me?"

"They seemed to think I had the right."

"Of course you do. I gave it to you when I said we were engaged. But somebody could have kept you company."

"You know that doesn't mean anything," she said with distress in her voice. "I feel like such a fraud. You really should tell Beau and Lance, at least."

"It might mean something if you let it."

She gave him a narrow look. "You don't know what you're saying, it must be the anesthesia. The last thing you want is a wife to interfere with your dirt bike races and football games."

"You don't know what I want."

"I know now is not the time to decide." She reached across him, aiming for the nurse call button. He caught her hand and turned it up so the facets on the ruby and diamond ring on her finger sparkled in the morning light. "You're still wearing this. And I seem to remember a kiss last night while I was half out of it, and a whisper that had something to do with love."

"Trey—"

"What? Tell me."

"I thought you might die, and the middle of that kind of crisis was no time to explain to your friends that our engagement was a farce."

"Is it? Is it really?"

She looked away from him, her chocolate-colored eyes incredibly dark. "It has to be. There are things you don't know."

"So tell me." Trey wasn't entirely sure he wanted to hear

it, but figured this was his best chance, while he had sympathy on his side.

"I don't think so, not right now. You were shot, for heaven sakes. You shouldn't be upset. Besides, you may not even remember next time you wake up."

"If not now, when, Zeni?"

She pulled her hand free of his grasp. Rising, she moved away to the window where she stood with her back to him. She adjusted the blinds to decrease the light, and then stood winding the cords around her fingers.

As the minutes stretched, impatience moved over him, lending strength to his voice. "You've been putting this off for days. I don't know what's so bad, but it can't be any worse than what I might lay here imagining."

"Your doctor won't like it, and I don't know if—"

"I'll be the judge of what I can stand and want to hear."

"Yes, but—are you sure?"

He let his silence answer for him.

"All right, fine." She didn't begin right away but looked out the window with a bleak expression, as if organizing her thoughts. When she finally spoke her manner was distant, a deliberate disassociation from what she was saying.

"I've told you a little about my mother. She was bright, well read, formed her own opinions, and did her best to leave her conservative upbringing behind when she left home. After I was born, she discovered she'd given birth to a math and science freak, a kid who understood long division before she could crawl and had an IQ of 150 before hitting her teens. Given my nerd tendencies and her artistic and liberal bent, the two of us never quite fit in—though it mattered less in the Quarter than it might have anywhere else. After she was gone, I went off the deep end for a while."

"Understandable," Trey said, even as he frowned at the bleak yet oddly recognizable picture she'd painted. He'd always known she was smart, but not that smart.

"Anyway, there was a man who lived with us when I was small, too small to remember much about him. All I know is that he was gentle, quiet spoken and had a musical lilt to his voice. I think he was a composer who wrote both lyrics and music, and sometimes played at one of the clubs on Bourbon Street—I can almost see his long fingers on the keys of an old piano. There was a song my mother used to sing—but that's not the point."

"He was your father?" Trey asked with some idea of helping her along.

"I think he may have been, though I'm not sure. My mother wasn't exactly forthcoming. She had men friends, but they never lived with us, and that made Jaze special."

"That was his name? And it's maybe on your birth certificate?"

"The space for the father's name was left blank."

Trey frowned at that, but let it go. "It sounds as if he didn't stick around long."

"Not by choice. He was killed coming home one night, stabbed during some kind of argument or robbery."

"That must have been tough."

"I suppose, though I was too little to know much about

it. My mother never talked about it, not even when I was old enough to be curious." She gave a small shrug. "I asked one of the Quarter policemen if it would be possible to look into it. He told me to let it lie, that there might be something I'd prefer not to know, maybe a drug connection or worse."

"But why—"

"Jaze was from Jamaica. He was also what's known as a quadroon."

That explained it. A quadroon, in New Orleans parlance, was a person with one quarter African American heritage and the remainder Caucasian. Regardless of the proportions, he'd have been identified as African American with all the racial profiling that implied.

"At least, that's what my mother told me, and I have a vague memory of playing with his dreadlocks."

The quiet in the room as she finished speaking was absolute. From the corridor outside came low voices and the click of high heels, along with the squeak of a passing medical cart and distant chimes signaling announcements. She was watching him, Trey knew, waiting to see his reaction. The best he could do was a shrug, though the movement brought such a burst of pain in his chest that it took his breath for a second.

"That's it?" he asked finally. "That's the big secret?"

Her smile had a twist to it. "Isn't it enough?"

"But you don't know if this Jaze guy was your father or a friend of your mother's, a hardened criminal or just a man who met bad luck one night."

"Exactly," she answered on a winded laugh. "Fatherless,

234 | JENNIFER BLAKE

motherless, penniless, that's me. My mother used to say the answer to it all was blowin' in the wind, but she couldn't chase it down, and I doubt I will, either."

"You haven't even tried. You mentioned grandparents before. Surely they can be located. They must know who your mother was involved with when she got pregnant."

Zeni dismissed that idea with a tired smile. "What does it matter? It's obvious I'm different. You said so yourself."

"Seems it matters to you." He paused, his eyes narrowed on her features, so lovely and yes, exotic. "Or does it? Maybe it's just an excuse to move on, let the wind blow you some place new. That's easier than staying and dealing with the truth."

"What do you know about it? You've always been sure of exactly who you are and where you belong. But I don't. Never have and never will."

The door swung open then on its hydraulic hinges. Derek Peabody strolled in as if there was no possible doubt of his welcome.

"Better listen to her Benedict. We can get a blood test to be sure about this interesting relationship you're discussing, but there's no doubt she's one of a kind, maybe another Halle Berry success story in the making. Or that she deserves better than a wasted life in this godforsaken spot on the map, if it comes to that. I'm here to see that she gets it."

CHAPTER NINETEEN

*A*larm coursed through Zeni's veins. Derek appeared to be unarmed and therefore non-threatening, but how could she tell? All she knew was that she didn't trust him. Nor was she happy to see Bettina clack her way into the room behind him with her expensive clipboard under her arm.

"What do you want?"

Moving to Trey's bedside at once, Zeni gripped its railing, making certain her fingers were poised over the integrated nurse call button.

"You, of course," Derek said on a laugh. "What else?"

Bettina laughed in mirthless sycophancy. "Direct, isn't he? But you might as well give in gracefully. Derek always gets what he wants."

"Zeni may have something to say about that," Trey said.

Glancing down at him, Zeni saw that he had put a hand

to his chest, while perspiration lay across his upper lip. Hesitating no longer, she pressed the call button. To the pair near the door she said, "Trey has talked enough for now. He's too weak for further discussion, but especially about something as unimportant as the movie. You need to leave."

"Unimportant?"

Bettina looked scandalized as she repeated that pertinent word. A pained expression crossed Derek's face, but that was all.

"In the present scheme of things, yes. Trey was nearly killed, as if you don't know. He doesn't need this."

At that moment, the voice of the duty nurse came over the intercom. "May I help you?"

"Yes," Zeni said clearly. "My fiancé needs something for pain as soon as possible."

The nurse said she would check his chart, and Zeni thanked her. Derek didn't speak until the intercom clicked off.

"Oh, really now, isn't that a bit obvious as a way to get someone in here, as well as being unnecessary?"

"You are a suspect, and as such—"

"Zeni," Trey said, a hint of warning in his voice. "I think—it's possible the shooter was targeting you. It seemed for a second there last night that you were in the line of fire."

She barely glanced at him. "If I was, it was an accident. I saw where the shots struck. I also saw that Derek and Bettina were not in the booth."

The actor straightened from his world-weary pose. "Wait a minute—"

"That being the case," she went on, meeting his gaze with determination since it seemed her job to protect Trey for a change, "I think the pair of you should leave before I call Sheriff Benedict."

"Charming. It's quite the cushy family enclave you've landed in here at Chamelot, isn't it?"

"Something it would be dangerous for you to forget."

"Ridiculous," Derek said with every sign of exasperation.

The nurse should be along with the pain medication at any moment, Zeni knew. At least Derek and Bettina were aware she would be arriving, so unlikely to try anything. "Trey should rest. You may come back later, if you must, but I'll walk you out now."

"Zeni," Trey said again, his voice hoarse.

She gave him a strained smile. "I'll be right back." She might or might not be, but he didn't need to worry either way.

She walked to the door and reached to hold it open. When Derek and his assistant passed out ahead of her, she closed it behind her. They had barely gone three steps when Derek touched her arm.

"You don't really think I had anything to do with this shooting?"

"I don't know, but someone did." She continued down the hall with determined strides, so he was forced to move beside her.

He actually looked puzzled and more than a little

disturbed. "But why? Why would I take such a chance?"

"How should I know? Maybe you thought having your way was more important than a man's life. Maybe you expected to get away with murder in such a small town."

A sardonic smile curved his famous mouth. "I like you, Zeni, and think you'd be great in the movie I'm making. I was looking forward to working—and playing—with you, and even thought it might be something special. But you are seriously mistaken if you think I care enough about getting into your pants to kill a man for it."

"Excuse me," Bettina said. "I just realized I put my clipboard down on the tray table back in the room. I'll run and get it."

Zeni barely glanced at the assistant as she clicked back down the hall in her stilettos. Her concentration was on Derek Peabody. She could almost swear he meant every word he'd said.

"I don't think for a minute that you care about me," she said. "You don't know me, after all. But you do care about your movie, and care even more about your ego. Trey not only blocked your way to getting into my pants, as you so gallantly put it, but he embarrassed you in front of your crew. That's something you'd find hard to forgive."

"Oh, come on! Let's not go overboard. Whoever shot Benedict probably didn't mean to kill him. I expect it was some kid showing off, or a gun-happy redneck he beat in one of his bike races. I'll forget you made these wild accusations, and we can get back to work. Filming on the dream sequence is scheduled for tomorrow. I'll expect to see you there."

"It isn't happening," Zeni said with precision. "Find yourself another Zenobia."

He stared at her, his expression so stunned that he looked witless. "You can't do this! I meant what I said back there. I can take you away from Chamelot. You could really go places, do great things."

"I'm not going anywhere, and have no interest in doing great things if it means pretending the rest of my life. Chamelot is real, and that suits me better than any make-believe." She turned away from him, but swung back again.

"You might try Gloria, the girl playing the handmaiden, as Zenobia. She'd probably enjoy being a Middle Eastern warrior queen if it helped to pay her college expenses."

Derek Peabody stood there watching her as she walked away. Zeni didn't look back.

She couldn't return to Trey's room fast enough. She hated that she'd had to leave him, especially when he was hurting, but walking Derek and Bettina out had seemed the fastest way to get rid of them.

The assistant should have been on her way back down the hall after retrieving her clipboard. She was nowhere in sight. What was she doing in Trey's room? What was she saying to him?

A dull, clanging thud like metal hitting the floor came to Zeni as she neared the door. She recognized it almost at once, knew it had to be the rolling table with Trey's breakfast that had been beside his bed. Following on it came the sharp sound of a woman's voice.

Zeni hit the door with her shoulder. She catapulted inside.

Bettina was bent over Trey's upper body with his pillow in her hands. She shrilled curses as she tried to hold it over his face while digging an elbow into his chest. He had her wrists clamped in his fists and was struggling to throw her aside. His breathing harsh, coming in labored gasps of pain. Coffee and milk spread across the floor, coming from his upended breakfast tray. The rolling table lay on its side beneath the window.

With a cry of rage, Zeni flung herself at the assistant. She grabbed her shoulder and a handful of bleached blonde hair, hauling her back.

Bettina grunted like a madwoman, kicking at her. Her stiletto caught Zeni in the knee. She stumbled back, slamming into the corner of the bathroom wall.

It was then the door whooshed open and the duty nurse appeared. In her hand was a tray with the syringe of powerful painkiller she'd ordered laid out upon it.

Zeni didn't think, didn't plan. She grabbed that syringe in her fist. With her thumb on the plunger, she whirled around and stabbed the needle into Bettina's neck. She pressed her thumb down with all her might.

The assistant screeched and grabbed for the injection site, her face a mask of horror. Zeni whisked the syringe away and jumped back while sickness rose inside her.

Trey batted away the pillow that half covered his face, wincing as he flung it from the bed. Eyes wide, he stared at Bettina, but quickly shifted his gaze to Zeni's face. His feature's cleared.

"Thank God," he whispered, and held out his hand.

She swallowed. He was okay. They were both okay.

Bettina was not. She crumpled, sliding down the side of the bed to land on her backside with a solid thud. Her eyes were wide with shock and her lips moved without sound.

Stepping around her with care, Zeni reached Trey's bedside. She put her hand in his, holding to its warm strength.

It was then that the duty nurse began to yell at all of them.

CHAPTER TWENTY

*I*t was over. The danger for Trey, the engagement, the part in the movie—all of it was over. Zeni knew that without question as she sat at Trey's bedside, yet she couldn't make herself get up and go.

She should leave, she really should—leave the hospital, leave the Watering Hole, leave Chamelot. To stay now would only make it harder to go in the end.

Yet who was going to look after Trey once he left the hospital? Who was going to manage the coffee shop and all his other enterprises until he could get back on his feet? She couldn't desert him when he needed her most.

Yes, he had his cousins and his friends, and they would be glad to take care of him. They didn't know him as she did, however, his likes and dislikes, how he wanted his coffee, his favorite brand of beer, how he liked his eggs and hamburgers and what he looked like when he was sleeping.

No. She would not think of the last. To remember how he'd kissed her, made love to her, and held her through their one night together was not going to help matters. If she let herself think about it too much she would never go at all.

She longed to stay. The need to know how Trey would have dealt with the uncertain race of her father and his possible criminal connections was an ache inside her. Her greatest fear, however, was that he intended to be gallant, to say it didn't matter when she knew it did—or very well could someday.

He didn't know she was there. He was asleep, all sign of pain smoothed from his features, his lashes casting shadows on his high cheekbones. The pain medication that she had put to such good use had been reordered and given as soon as his doctor was certain there had been no real damage from his struggle with Bettina. Trey had accepted it without complaint because he knew the danger was at an end and she was safe.

Zeni closed her eyes and shook her head, trying to banish the scene that played out in her mind again and yet again: the hospital room in chaos, Bettina looking murderous as she tried to smother Trey, the nurse appearing in the door with the prepared syringe. It was over; the room restored to order. It was over; but she still felt the effects like the sting of acid in her veins.

She had wanted to kill Derek's assistant. It was only blind luck that she had not, that the syringe hadn't struck an artery, sending the powerful painkiller directly to

244 | JENNIFER BLAKE

Bettina's heart. Zeni was glad now, but on first hearing the woman would live, she had felt nothing but burning regret.

That had been several hours ago. Bettina had been taken away after being examined. What became of her, Zeni didn't know.

The door of the room swung open, letting in the brighter light from the corridor. Zeni looked up, every sense alert.

It was a different nurse, gray-haired and kindly. "Just checking to be sure everything is okay, hon," she said with professional quiet.

"He's fine."

"Yes, I see that. He's fortunate to have you. Now is there anything you need, anything I can get you?"

Better willpower, maybe, or a new heart? They didn't have those down at the nurse's station.

Zeni shook her head.

"There are a couple of people out here who would like to step inside a minute, if it's all right with you."

Zeni wasn't sure when she'd become Trey's guardian, but it didn't matter. "Fine, as long as they don't wake him."

"No problem. I told them that, but they knew already." She turned away to motion to someone out of sight, and then vanished into the hall.

It was Mandy who put her head around the door, though she was quickly followed by Lance, Beau and Carla. Without stopping, Lance's wife came toward Zeni with her arms outstretched.

"Oh my God, sweetie!" she said, folding her into a full warm embrace. "I can't believe you, taking on that crazy woman all by yourself. And putting her away, too!"

Zeni managed a smile that was, truth to tell, a little watery. "Well, Trey did have her by both wrists."

"Big deal." Carla wrapped her arms around both Zeni and Mandy for a group hug. "You sure you're all right?"

"Absolutely," she answered, looking from one to another of the visitors as she emerged from the shelter of their arms. "But I was just sitting here wondering what happened to Bettina when they took her out of here."

"They didn't tell you?" Mandy gave her husband a look that held more than a little disbelief. "Lance took her into custody once the doctor was done with her. Right now, she's sleeping off the painkiller in a cell. When she wakes up she'll be charged with attempted murder, assault and reckless endangerment, plus a few other things. That should put her away for a long while."

"Good." Zeni didn't want to show her relief too obviously, but that didn't mean it wasn't heartfelt.

"Good is right," Carla echoed. "Though I have to say, I don't understand what she thought she was doing. I mean, I could see Derek going after Trey if he'd set his sights on you. He seems to be a petty, vindictive guy with a massive ego and overdeveloped sense of entitlement. But what was this Bettina going to gain? They were involved, or so everyone said. Why would she try to get rid of your fiancé?"

"She and Derek both said it was her job to make sure he had whatever he wanted," Zeni answered, since she'd had time to think about it. "If you carry that to its logical conclusion—"

246 | JENNIFER BLAKE

"Or, in her case, the illogical one?" Mandy put in.

Beau, watching them, used his thumb to scratch at his scruff of golden-brown beard. "It sounds extreme."

"She hasn't been a model citizen since *Rifle Fire* was canceled," Lance said. "A background check brought up drug issues, mental health issues, and credit card fraud with a couple of aliases. I'd say Peabody is lucky she never went after him with a rifle—or a pillow."

"I should say so," Mandy said, "especially with the rifle. I remember her handling one like a pro as Derek's co-star on his hit show."

"*Rifle Fire*, yeah," Beau said. "But did Peabody have no responsibility in all this?"

Carla understood what her husband was driving at before anyone else. "You mean, is it possible he put Bettina up to it? He may be a horse's behind, but it doesn't follow that he'd incite anyone to murder."

"I do know women can think and act for themselves," Beau told her with a flashing grin. "But that he was the driving force is not impossible."

"Which is why I'll be discussing it with her when she wakes up, certainly before Derek takes himself out of town," Lance said.

"Good plan." Zeni meant that exactly as it sounded.

"And if you're wondering when darling Derek and his movie company will be gone," Carla told Zeni, "it seems he and his crew will finish the scenes they have laid out, but everything else will be filmed on a Hollywood soundstage. They should be packed up and out of town by the end of next week."

That also sounded like a good plan. It was, just possibly, one she might follow up on herself if Trey was up and around by then. Not that she'd be going anywhere near Hollywood, but Trey didn't need to know that, and might never find out if she was careful.

"Anyway," Mandy said, her gaze a bit too knowing as she looked at Zeni, "we came to see about you as well as Trey. We've all had a chance to go home, take a shower and rest a bit, while you've been here since last night—"

"Last night?" Zeni glanced at the window, and was surprised to see the light outside was fading, the last of the sunlight slanting toward evening.

"It's lovely that you've been so dedicated, but you can't hold out forever. Lance and Beau will stay with Trey tonight, and Mandy and I will drive you to your apartment. You can get some rest then we'll all put our heads together and decide what's best for Trey."

It seemed she wasn't the only one who could make arrangements.

Zeni slept the clock around. She'd heard that phrase before but never actually done it. It was hard to believe so much time had passed with no one disturbing her, but the reason soon became clear. Gloria had dared anyone to step foot on the stairs to her apartment, and kept the noise level down in the coffee shop as well.

It was almost noon before she rolled out of bed and went in search of coffee. She'd been too keyed up to sleep when she first came in; that was on top of running the gauntlet of the Watering Hole's customers. Everyone was concerned and curious, and no one wanted their news second hand, not when she was in sight. It had been after eleven before she was able to close her eyes, also after she'd fed and petted Midnight, took a hot bath while drinking a couple of glasses of wine, and downloaded a dull book on how to overcome insomnia. Once she finally relaxed, however, it was like falling over a cliff and never hitting the bottom.

Now that she was awake and something close to her normal self again, she was able to think more clearly than the evening before. Facing Trey and letting him know what was on her mind had never been a problem; she only dreaded it now because it mattered so much. So it might be painful, so what? Running away as she'd imagined wouldn't be fair to either of them.

There was no point in putting it off. Besides, she wanted to see him. If he was awake, he must be wondering what had become of her. Or maybe not, as the others had surely told him. Anyway, she was going to the hospital if she had to retrieve his Harley from the arena and ride it to get there.

She showered, found something to eat, and skimmed into the black pants and white shirt that were the most subdued things she owned. She brushed her hair until it shone and, wryly amused at her Southern belle type primping, applied mascara, lip-gloss, and a coating of concealer for the shadows that still lay under her eyes.

When she was done, she looked normal. Amazingly enough, she didn't mind. Trey knew the worst; she no longer had any need to hide anything from him. And no one else really mattered.

She walked out of the bedroom, headed toward her shoulder bag that she'd left on the chest in front of the sofa. At a small sound from the entrance door, she glanced up.

Trey stood framed in the opening, his hands in his pockets while he rested one shoulder against the frame. How he'd come to be there was no great mystery; it was his building so he must have had an extra key.

"Headed somewhere?"

She closed her open mouth with a snap. "To the hospital. What are you doing out of it?"

"Doc said I was good to go, as long as I'm careful. The place I wanted to go was here."

A shiver ran over her at the words, but she refused to hold his gaze. "You should be at home in bed."

"Good idea, if you'd care to join me."

"Don't."

"No, not such a good idea, after all." His smile was wry. "But we have some unfinished business."

She looked at him then, seeing the concern and determination in the gray depths of his eyes. A silent sigh left her. "I suppose we do. Come in and sit down before you fall down. Is there anything I can get you, coffee, water, pie or something else to eat that isn't hospital food?"

"I'm good."

He did seem to be, as he moved to the couch and sank down on it. He might move a little gingerly, look a little pale, but no one would guess that he'd been shot if they didn't know it.

250 | JENNIFER BLAKE

As she went to close the door behind him, she tried to marshal her thoughts, to decide what she was going to say. It was impossible until she knew exactly what he meant by coming to her apartment. There was one thing she could do, however.

Removing the ruby and diamond ring that he had bought for her, holding it clenched in her hand for a second, she stepped to the coffee table and put it down in front of him. Retreating at once, she took the chair that sat at an angle from the couch.

"What's this?" He stared down at the ring, but didn't pick it up.

"You know very well. With Derek pulling in his horns and getting ready to leave town, there's no longer a need for our pretend engagement."

"What if we forget the pretend part and make it real?" Midnight glided from the bedroom and leaped up beside him, and Trey smoothed a hand down his back, watching what he was doing instead of looking at her.

"I told you why there at the hospital yesterday. Unless you don't remember?"

Anger turned his eyes storm-cloud gray as he glanced up. "I remember. What I don't recall is getting an answer to the question of whether you're going or staying."

"I-I can't stay."

"Why not? You think you'll find whatever it is you're looking for at the next town down the road? It's here, right in front of you, and you can't or won't see it."

"I'm the one who needs to decide that."

"I agree," he said a shade too promptly. "You have to decide who you want to be and where you want to stay, and then do it and be damned to everyone else. I just don't see that who your father might have been makes any difference."

"Of course you do, or should. You're a Benedict. Your family has been here since the flood. You and your cousins are old-time Chamelot with the old family plantation houses to prove it. You don't want to take the chance that your children might be laughed at or slighted because they're—different."

"For God's sake, Zeni, how can you sit there and say that? You have an IQ of 150, and mine is not nearly that high. Could you take the chance, even though our children might not be extra bright?"

"It's not the same thing," she said with a quick shake of her head.

"I say it is," he insisted. "More than that, I'll tell you something about this famous Benedict family you think is so aristocratic. It started in Tunica Parish with four brothers who had migrated west out of Virginia by way of Georgia and Mississippi. They didn't wind up here in the back of beyond, a primitive wilderness at the time, simply because they found rich bottom land along the river. Oh, no. According to stories handed down in the family, they were running from something—God knows what, but probably a killing, accidental or otherwise. They'd picked up some interesting women along the way, too. One was a black-haired Native American, and another a misunderstood blonde, beautiful but no better than she had to be for good and various reasons. There was a Spanish female with a temper and a little knife she'd used once too often, and a Frenchwoman who'd made a career of marrying sickly older men—until she met a Benedict who was hale and hearty. About the best you can say for the whole crew is that they were strong, hardworking and ready to take whatever risks might be necessary to have a new and better life."

"You're making that up." She was almost certain of it, though she wanted to believe him, longed to with every ounce of her being.

"Why would I do that?"

"You know why. Besides, it was long ago."

"So is whatever happened in your family."

She brushed that away with a quick gesture of one hand. "But the Benedicts are respected members of the community now. The name stands for stability and integrity and all the old-fashioned values that are so hard to find."

"And you're going to be all noble and refuse to marry me because of it, and because of something that might or might not be true about your family? Well, thank you very much."

"Oh, is that supposed to be your part in all this?" she demanded as her annoyance rose with his accusation. "You're going to be *all noble* and marry me in spite of it?"

"I want to marry you because I love you, Zeni, and I don't take kindly to this idea of yours that I must be unable to accept your birth, whatever it might be, because I'm a Southern country boy."

"I never said—"

"It seemed that way to me."

She tightened her hands into fists, heartsick at arguing with him about something so personal, yet unable to stop. "Maybe it was, but a lot of people do think that way."

"Some do, yes. But I'll remind you that not everyone, or even every Southerner, is the same. You can't judge a man by where he was born or how. No, and not by the vocal few whose brains are stuck back in the nineteenth century with their dead ancestors, and who never had an independent thought in their lives. This is the twenty-first century America, Zeni. Every single one of us is the child of an immigrant and a fine mixture of races and colors and wild-haired genes after thousands of years of population movements and enemy invasions. More than that, it's been proven that we each and every one come from the same hot savannah in Africa. What the devil difference does it make what the color of our hair and skin might be? It's what's in our hearts that matters."

"Oh, Trey." She could barely see him for the tears that welled into her eyes, rising from the deep sense of healing inside her. He was such an unusual man, honest and compassionate, strong and true and, most of all, fair. She loved him beyond all thought, loved him enough to give him up if it was the best thing for him.

But if not? If it truly wasn't best, what then?

"Marry me, Zeni," he said, moving to kneel beside her chair, taking her hand and placing in her palm the antique ruby and diamond ring that stood for her heart and his protection of it. "Please marry me and help me name my granddad's old house and turn it into a home. Help me build a life worth having. Marry me and have my children."

"Are you sure? Are you really sure?"

"I was never more certain of anything in my life," he said in deep avowal. "You are my life and the only future I need, the rose I yearn for despite its thorns. I love you more than I can say, need you beside me, want you in my heart for all the days of our lives. That is, if you meant what you whispered when you thought I might be dying, if you can always love me."

"Yes," she whispered, closing her fingers tight on his ring. "Yes. Oh, please yes."

He joined her in her chair, taking her on his lap. She melted into him with gentle care for his injury, pushing her fingers into his hair as he took her mouth, her throat, pressing his face into her neck so she felt the moisture from his eyes, and then taking his mouth again for a kiss flavored with the salt of her own tears. Touching, holding in an agony of relief and promise, they came together in peace at last.

It was later, much later, when Zeni sighed and shifted, resting her forehead against his jawbone while he cupped her breast, his hand disappearing inside the open placket of her shirt.

"There's something else I have to tell you," she said, her voice musing and contented, yet just a tiny bit smug.

"What's that?" he asked, his concentration elsewhere.

"The gene for intelligence is inherited through the mother's DNA."

His movement stilled. "What does that mean?"

"Why, only that our children will be of strong Benedict stock with all those good healthy genes, but they should also be bright, very bright indeed."

"So my logic was all wrong?"

"I didn't say that. It's just that, well—these children of ours should be awesome."

His hold upon her tightened, became caressing. "They will be. And I can't wait to see. I really can't wait."

END

Did you miss any of the other
LOUISIANA KNIGHTS romances?

LANCELOT OF THE PINES
(Book 1 in The Louisiana Knights Series)

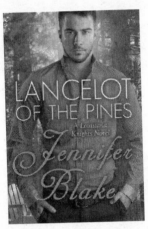

CHIVALRY LIVES IN THE SULTRY SOUTH!

Mandy wants only to be left alone; she knows nothing about the disappearance of her much older husband, and less about the thug who tried to abduct her. Forced to hide out in a backwater town, the last thing she needs is an overbearing deputy's protection.

Lance, saddled with the protective instinct that goes with the name of Arthur's most trusted knight, is stunned by his reaction to Mandy's courage and beauty. But is he putting his life on the line for an innocent in danger—or for a Black Widow?

GALAHAD IN JEANS
(Book 2 in The Louisiana Knights Series)

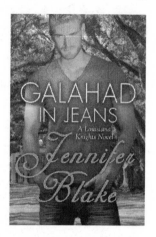

It was payback, assigning Carla the job of writing the profile for her magazine's Perfect Southern Gentleman contest winner; her boss knows she thinks the Southern Gentleman is a myth. So she's supposed to do a hatchet job on this Redneck Romeo? Fine, she can handle it.

Beau would avoid the starchy lady editor and her magazine feature if he hadn't promised to cooperate; he's an ordinary guy, no matter how often the townsfolk set him up as a hero. Yet the closer he gets to Carla, the more he'd like to be the gentleman she needs....

CHRISTMAS KNIGHT
(A Louisiana Knights Holiday Novella)

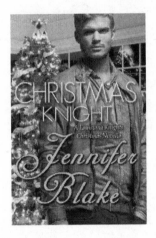

Home health nurse Donna Ingraham is determined to give her elderly patient, Granny Chauvin, the kind of real Christmas tree she recalls from the past. Hatchet in hand, Donna sets out to cut down the perfect specimen from an abandoned property.

Only the place's brand-new owner, Jake Benedict, has earmarked the tree she's eyeing for his special family party. And if he remembers the fiery kiss they shared as teenagers, he's not letting on.

A freak accident involving Jake's motorcycle, a rabbit and that sharp hatchet makes Donna's first aid skill necessary. In return, Jake feels obliged to share his tree. Will he and Donna will be sharing something more by Christmas Eve?

About the Author

National and international bestselling author Jennifer Blake is a charter member of Romance Writers of America and recipient of the RWA Lifetime Achievement Award. She hold numerous other honors, including the "Maggie", the Holt Medallion, Reviewer's Choice, Pioneer and Career Achievement Awards from *RT Book Reviews Magazine*, and the Frank Waters Award for literary excellence. She has written 73 books with translations in 22 languages and more than 35 million copies in print worldwide.

After three decades in traditional publishing, Jennifer established Steel Magnolia Press LLC with Phoenix Sullivan in 2011. This independent publishing company now publishes her work.

FMI: http://www.jenniferblake.com.

You can also find Jennifer on Facebook, Twitter, and Pinterest.

Find Jennifer's books on Amazon at
http://www.amazon.com/Jennifer-Blake/e/B000APHHS8

More Titles by Jennifer Blake

Louisiana Knights Series
Lancelot of the Pines
Galahad in Jeans
Tristan on a Harley
Christmas Knight *(A Holiday Novella)*

Contemporary Romance
The Tuscan's Revenge Wedding
The Venetian's Daring Seduction
The Amalfitano's Bold Abduction
Holding the Tigress
Shameless
Wildest Dreams
Joy and Anger
Love and Smoke

Sweet Contemporary Romance
April of Enchantment
Captive Kisses
Love at Sea
Snowbound Heart
Bayou Bride
The Abducted Heart

Historical Romance
Silver-Tongued Devil
Arrow to the Heart
Spanish Serenade
Perfume of Paradise
Southern Rapture
Louisiana Dawn
Prisoner of Desire
Royal Passion
Fierce Eden
Midnight Waltz
Surrender In Moonlight
Royal Seduction
Embrace and Conquer
Golden Fancy
The Storm and the Splendor
Tender Betrayal
Notorious Angel
Love's Wild Desire
Sweet Piracy

Romantic Suspense
Night of the Candles
Bride of a Stranger
Dark Masquerade
Court of the Thorn Tree
The Bewitching Grace
Stranger at Plantation Inn
Secret of Mirror House

eBOOKS:

Box Sets
Contemporary Collection Volume 1
Contemporary Collection Volume 2
Classic Gothics Collection Volume 1
Classic Gothics Collection Volume 2
Italian Billionaire's TwinPack
Louisiana History Collection Volume 1
Louisiana History Collection Volume 2
Love and Adventure Collection Volume 1
Love and Adventure Collection Volume 2
Louisiana Plantation Collection
No Ordinary Lovers
Royal Princes of Ruthenia
Sweetly Contemporary Collection Volume 1
Sweetly Contemporary Collection Volume 2

Nonfiction
Around the World in 100 Days (with Corey Faucheux)

Novellas
Queen for a Night
A Vision of Sugarplums
Pieces of Dreams
Out of the Dark
The Rent-A-Groom
The Warlock's Daughter
Besieged Heart
Dream Lover

Contact Jennifer Here:
Jenniferblake001@bellsouth.net

Or follow her here:
http://jenniferblake.com
https://www.facebook.com/jennifer.blake.3914
https://twitter.com/JenniferBlake01
http://www.pinterest.com/jblakeauthor
http://www.amazon.com/Jennifer-Blake/e/B000APHHS8

Made in the USA
Middletown, DE
29 August 2017